troubled spirit

River Heights' local psychic, Lucia Gonzalvo, was sitting at the circular table draped in black velvet. Several tarot cards were arranged in a pattern before her. Her fingertips rested on a card featuring a skeleton dressed in armor riding on a horse. Beneath the horse's hooves, DEATH was spelled out in capital letters.

"Nancy, hello," she said in her exotic accent. "I need to talk to you." She gestured to the cards. "I've been getting vibes all day that you should stay away from Hackett Mansion. That there's danger there." Her voice lowered. "That it is truly haunted and the spirit who walks there is troubled."

NANCY DREW

Available from Aladdin Paperbacks

CAROLYN KEENE

NANCY DREW

GIRL DETECTIVE®

ghost stories

CAROLYN KEENE

Aladdin Paperbacks
New York   London   Toronto   Sydney

❧ ALADDIN PAPERBACKS
An imprint of Simon & Schuster Children's Publishing Division
1230 Avenue of the Americas, New York, NY 10020
Copyright © 2008 by Simon & Schuster, Inc.
All rights reserved, including the right of
reproduction in whole or in part in any form.
NANCY DREW, NANCY DREW: GIRL DETECTIVE, ALADDIN PAPER-
BACKS, and related logo are registered trademarks of Simon & Schuster, Inc.
Manufactured in the United States of America
First Aladdin Paperbacks edition August 2008
10   9   8
Library of Congress Control Number 2007934379
ISBN-13: 978-1-4169-5909-0
ISBN-10: 1-4169-5909-2
0212 OFF

contents

manga mayhem

"So what do you think, Nancy?"

"Huh?" I blurted, nearly jumping out of my skin. "I mean, what?"

My dad chuckled as he escorted George, Bess, and me into our beautiful room at the Sakura Hotel in bright, bustling Tokyo. Bess Marvin and George Fayne, who were cousins, as well as my best friends, grinned and knowingly shook their heads.

"Something tells me you have no idea what we've been talking about," George drawled. "In fact, there's no mystery about it." She was such a kidder.

"True," I confessed. In fact, my brain was furiously working on a mystery of my own—the mystery of the Ghost Warriors. I had tuned out everything, including—I now realized—our train ride from Narita Airport to Ueno Station, and our taxi ride from the train station to the Sakura. I was really sorry I had missed it. At least I hadn't been driving; we would have probably run out of gas.

Things like that happen to me when I'm in the middle of a case—and I was dead center in a really good one. Emphasis on *dead*. *Ghost Warriors* was the spookiest ghost story/mystery I'd read in my entire life. And that's saying something since I'm a mystery solver and a fan of ghost stories.

"I just wanted to wish you a good night," my dad explained.

"Thanks, Mr. Drew. And thanks again for bringing us along," Bess replied. She looked as fresh as when we had driven into the Chicago airport nearly fifteen hours ago, every blond hair in place, her blue eyes lightly ringed with smudge-free mascara.

"Yes, thank you," George added, yawning as she ran her fingers through her short-cropped dark hair.

"You want a little light reading for bed?" I asked him, plucking the most recent copy of *Ghost Warriors* out of my bag. "Since it's Exhibit A?"

It was also the object of my "mystery-dar," which had been clanging ever since Janelle Stacy sent my dad the last three years of the *Ghost Warriors* manga in English. Ms. Stacy was a rising young executive at a major Hollywood talent agency, put in charge of her first huge deal—to expand *Ghost Warriors*, the most popular manga in the world, into a major international brand—with a TV show, feature movies, and tons of merchandise to sell to fans all over the world.

We met her on a trip to Hollywood and, as luck would have it, my dad had gone to college with Kenji McCarthy, the very man who was threatening to sue the creator of *Ghost Warriors*. If he went through with the suit, it would probably cost Ms. Stacy her job. So she asked my dad to travel to Japan to see if he could find a way to talk him out of it.

I had never thought of myself as a big manga reader, but when I skimmed a couple of issues of *Ghost Warriors* so I could help my dad with his legal briefs, I saw that it featured a cool mystery and a direct challenge to the reader to solve it. Then the next issue contained another mystery.

Who knew *Ghost Warriors* was so addictive? As soon as I figured out the answer to one mystery, the writers would introduce another one. And of course, there was a central mystery running throughout the entire series: how the loyal Ghost

Warriors could stop Oishi, their leader, from becoming evil, while at the same time avenging the death of their samurai master, Lord Asano.

But finally the answer was about to be revealed. The producers of *Ghost Warriors* were running a contest on their website for the best solution. The prize was a trip to Matsumoto Studios. Next they would introduce a new, long-running story line, just in time—or so they hoped—for *Ghost Warriors*'s splashy international debut.

Since my dad was involved, I couldn't enter the contest, but that didn't stop me from trying to prove my super sleuthing abilities!

"I wouldn't dream of parting you from *Ghost Warriors*," my dad said. "I'll see you all in the morning."

My dad left to go down the hall to his own room, and we three skirted around the two large beds covered with embroidered gold bedspreads, past a little table set up for tea, and ran to the panorama window that revealed thousands of skyscrapers and glittering lights.

"We're in Japan!" George pressed her nose against the glass. "Home of state-of-the-art, high-tech gadgets!"

"We're in *Tokyo*," Bess added, pretending to paw the window. "Home of beautiful fashions."

"We're in the land of the Ghost Warriors," I added, grinning.

"Nancy Drew, come back to us, come now," Bess teased me, waggling her fingers in my direction. "Let's plan our day. First thing in the morning, we'll check out Akihabara, where the electronics live, for George; then we can go to the Ginza shopping district for me. Let's see some historical sights too."

"Bess, I'm the family athlete, and I'm here to tell you that you can*not* do all that in one day," George informed her.

"Taxis, girls," Bess said. "Tokyo is famous for them. They never get lost, ever, and they're cheap."

"Nothing in Tokyo is cheap," George argued.

They chattered on. I was about to join in—I was really excited to be in Japan—but something steered my attention over to an alcove where two white satin chairs faced a flat-screen TV. On the glass table between the chairs sat a bulky brown package addressed to NANCY DREW. I picked it up and ripped it open.

It was the next issue of *Ghost Warriors*!

There was a small card inside, complete with the ghost warrior logo—a legion of blurry samurai against a full moon—and a name: YUKI Z.

Dear Nancy-san,

Welcome to Japan. I am Yuki. I work for Mr. Matsumoto. Please enjoy Ghost Warriors: The Two Warlords Collide.

With the best wishes of Matsumoto Studios,
Yuki Z.

"Wow!" I cheered.

Eagerly, I showed my present to the cousins. Bess smiled as she turned the page of *Shopping in Tokyo*, and George, who had just opened up her laptop to link to an interactive Tokyo map, nodded and gave me a thumbs-up.

I sat down in my rumpled travel clothes, meaning to just take a brief look at the new book, but soon I found myself reading *The Two Warlords Collide* without looking up once.

"We've lost her now," Bess said. "I'm going to hang up my clothes. I want to minimize the wrinkles."

"Me too," George said. "I hate living out of a suitcase."

"Have fun," I said vaguely.

Seconds later, I had practically forgotten they were there. The first panel of the manga was a chilling image of sinister Kira Castle on a craggy mountaintop. In the foreground, a samurai helmet decorated with the Ghost Warrior crest gleamed eerily in the moonlight. Oishi's hand rested on it.

In the next panel, his transformation into an evil ghost was progressing—stark white skin, round circles under his red, glowing eyes. I wondered if the helmet beam had some kind of evil transformation ray. Lady Mariko's transparent image hovered in the background beneath the cloud-choked moon. Did she have something to do with it?

I turned page after page, losing myself completely in the story, saying "hmm" when George or Bess spoke to me. After fewer than ten pages, the cousins turned out the lights to go to bed. Luckily, there was a small lamp on the table.

I was about a third of the way through the story when I felt my head bouncing against my chest and realized my eyes were closed. I forced them open, more asleep than awake. The hair prickled on the back of my neck. Suddenly I felt as though I was being watched. I turned my head, looked at the vast panorama window, and almost jumped out of my skin.

For an instant, I saw *another* face in the glass! It was white, with long, wild, white hair pulled up into a topknot and dark rings under its glowing red eyes, like the face of evil Oishi.

"Stop them," I heard a voice whisper.

Just as quickly as the white face had appeared, it vanished. A chill ran down my spine. I almost called out to the cousins to wake up. But I reminded myself I was probably still half-asleep, that my imagination had just gotten the better of me. After all, we were seventeen stories up in the middle of Tokyo, and there was no way *anyone* could have been outside my hotel room looking in.

Right?

In the morning, after a lavish Western-style breakfast of omelets, bacon, French toast, and coffee, my dad told us that Mr. Matsumoto had offered to give us a tour of his studio. I couldn't believe it! Even Bess and George decided to put their tourist plans on hold so they could tag along.

Mr. Matsumoto sent a limo for us and we all piled in, giggling and investigating the many cool accessories we found: a TV, complete game system, and lots of sodas and snacks. My dad had brought a large box of legal papers with him, and as soon as he sat down, he began poring over them.

"How's it going?" I asked him sympathetically.

He sighed. "Kenji McCarthy seems to have waited until *Ghost Warriors* gained worldwide

10

recognition before he threatened to sue," he said. "Now Ichiro Matsumoto has more to lose and might be more willing to settle."

George made a face. "Poor Mr. Matsumoto. I'd freak out if someone tried to sue me."

"It can be very frightening," my dad agreed. "We're talking about hundreds of millions of dollars."

Bess's and George's eyes widened.

"That's why Ms. Stacy needed a good lawyer," I chimed in, grinning with pride at my father. "Carson Drew is a force to be reckoned with."

"I appreciate the vote of confidence," my dad said. "I just hope I can persuade Ken and Ichiro Matsumoto to sit down and talk this over."

We had only gone a few blocks when the limo pulled off the street and the chauffeur hopped out to open our door. Given the extreme traffic in Tokyo, it would have been easier and quicker to walk. But the sky was gray, threatening rain, and a cold wind whipped my coat around my legs—I was glad we'd had shelter from the weather.

The building housing Matsumoto Studios rose over our heads. It wasn't as tall as the Sakura Hotel, but it was definitely a high-rise. There was a large statute of Oishi guarding the revolving entry door outside. Clouds obscured the weak daylight, hiding his face in shadow. I could imagine his eyes following us as we went inside—just as I had imagined them staring at me last night through the window.

Cut it out, I told myself. It's just a comic book!

Inside the lobby, which was decorated with brick and brass, I spotted a slender Japanese woman with close-cropped purple hair, a nose ring, and more dangly earrings than I could count, one of which was large and black. She wore a black *Ghost Warriors* T-shirt and a short purple skirt over ruffled red petticoats, a pair of black-and-purple striped tights, and red ballet slippers. She was talking to a man in a blue uniform and a white helmet. When she saw us, she bowed to him, and rushed over to us.

"Good morning, *ohayo gozaimasu*," she said. "I am Yuki Z. I'm so sorry, but this is a terrible time for us." She bowed again. "Someone has broken into our offices!"

"Would it be better if we came back later?" my father asked, sounding concerned.

She shook her head. "The police are finished." She gestured to the man she'd been talking to. "He is leaving now." The officer looked very different from Chief McGinnis, head of the River Heights PD.

As if on cue, the police officer inclined his head at us, then headed for the revolving door. Yuki touched her black earring and spoke in rapid Japanese. I realized the "earring" was a phone.

A short time later, a brass door at the back of the lobby opened and a tall, thin man with high cheekbones, dark eyes, and spiky, black-and-gray hair emerged. He was dressed in a black silk shirt, charcoal trousers, and black loafers.

"Drew-*san*, ladies, welcome to Japan. I am Matsumoto." My dad had explained to us that in Japanese, adding *san* at the end of someone's name was a gesture of politeness. You didn't add *san* to your own name because that was considered arrogant.

The man bowed to each of us, and we all bowed back in turn. I noticed that Mr. Matsumoto looked harried, his forehead etched with frown lines. "Someone broke into our building last night."

"I'm so sorry. Are you sure we shouldn't come back another time?" my father asked.

"No," Mr. Matsumoto replied. "We have everything under control."

"Do the police have any suspects?" I piped up.

"My daughter is something of an amateur detective," my father explained.

That seemed to catch Mr. Matsumoto off guard. He looked at me, then shook his head and pulled at the tips of his spiked hair.

"No, they have no suspects," he replied. His worry lines deepened and his eyes narrowed. "But I do."

Mr. Matsumoto led the way to the elevator, and my dad followed, looking troubled. "The Ken McCarthy I knew in college would never vandalize anyone's property," he said.

"People change, Drew-*san*," Mr. Matsumoto said.

For some silly reason, I thought about Oishi and my creepy dream from the night before. Even by the light of day, it still seemed so real.

The elevator door shut and Yuki pressed a button shaped like an *M*. When the doors opened again, they opened into an enormous, airy room as big as a cavern. The tile floor was covered with a maze of cubicles and the air was humming with excited voices.

"It's like the Batcave," George whispered dryly.

I saw a group of people, mostly men, in the standard computer programmer's uniform of a colorful T-shirt and jeans, gathered around what looked like a large scanner. There were piles of ripped paper all over the floor. Behind the machine, Japanese graffiti had been sprayed in red over colorful wall-sized graphics of the main characters of *Ghost Warriors*. I took a step forward to study the wall more closely, but Mr. Matsumoto held up a hand.

"I'm sorry, but I must ask that no one touches that," he said.

"Oh, okay." I stepped back and made an awkward little bow, trying to be a polite visitor. "What does it say, if you don't mind my asking?"

"It is the Forty-Seven Ronin," Yuki whispered, seeing the graffiti. "They have struck again!" Her eyes shone and I really couldn't tell if she was frightened or thrilled. Maybe a bit of both.

"Yuki, I believe you have work," Mr. Matsumoto said tiredly.

"Yes, Matsumoto-*san*." She bowed low to all of us and turned away.

Mr. Matsumoto watched her with a strange expression, looking from her retreating form to the graffiti and back again. That was interesting.

"Is Yuki your secretary?" I asked.

"No," he said. "Yuki's my publicist."

"What was she saying about the Forty-Seven Ronin?" George blurted out. Bess nudged her with her elbow, but George didn't even blink.

Mr. Matsumoto sighed. "There are rumors all

over the Internet that the ghosts themselves want us to stop telling their story," he explained.

"What does the graffiti say?" I asked.

He looked at the wall. "This reads, 'We, the Forty-Seven Ronin, are the original Ghost Warriors. We demand that you stop exploiting our story for financial gain.'"

"And you think Yuki is planting these rumors?" my dad asked, saying exactly what I was thinking.

"I don't know. She denies it. But the controversy has created a lot of publicity," Mr. Matsumoto admitted.

There's an old saying that any publicity is good publicity, I thought.

"So nothing was taken?" I asked. "What about your equipment? Was anything damaged?"

Mr. Matsumoto chuckled. "You are a very curious young woman."

"You have no idea," George said under her breath. Bess grinned.

"I hope I'm not asking too many questions," I replied. "It's kind of a habit." After all, it's hard to solve mysteries if you don't ask any questions. And this was an even more intriguing mystery than the ones within the pages of *Ghost Warriors*.

As Bess, George, and I trailed after my dad and

Mr. Matsumoto, I took one more glance over my shoulder. Yuki had joined the group that was gathered around the machine, and she was talking earnestly to a handsome man with a goatee and a freckled, turned-up nose. He nodded and kept his head down, fumbling with some paper. He looked nervous.

"Hayashi-*san*," Mr. Matsumoto said, stopping. He gestured for the man with the goatee to come over. The man—Hayashi-*san*—paled as he bobbed his head and approached. Yuki pretended to pick up papers, but I noticed that she was watching Hayashi-*san* carefully as he approached his boss.

Hmmm.

"This is Taro Hayashi," he said. "He's one of our most promising artists. He has recently been promoted to our conceptual design department. In fact, he created Lady Mariko."

"Really?" I said. "I love Lady Mariko! I think she's going to save Oishi from turning evil. Am I even close?"

"Ah!" Taro said, his eyes lighting up. "You are a fan?"

"Yes." I grinned at him. "A huge fan." I reached into my large satchel-purse combo and pulled out my copy of *The Two Warlords Collide*. "Am I right about the mystery?" I asked again.

"You'll have to wait and see," he said mysteriously.

"Thank you for asking Yuki to send this to me," I said belatedly to Mr. Matsumoto. He bowed.

"Taro-*san*, would you autograph this for me?"

"Oh, I . . ." Taro blushed. "I'm just part of the team. . . ."

"Taro is very shy," Mr. Matsumoto explained.

"Here," I said, grabbing a pen out of my purse and handing it to Taro.

He signed the cover of my book, then bowed and held the pen out to me. His hand was trembling slightly. I noticed that his right pinkie was curved slightly, as if it had been broken a long time ago and hadn't healed properly.

"Thank you so much," I told him.

"It's my pleasure." He bowed to me and then to his boss. "Thank you," he said, and darted away like a scared rabbit.

Mr. Matsumoto opened a door that led into what looked like a conference room. The room was dominated by a black rectangular table that was lined with red chairs. A young woman dressed in a business suit greeted us with a tray of steamy teacups as Mr. Matsumoto invited us to sit down and then pulled out a seat for my father, too. Everyone sat and sipped his or her tea.

Mr. Matsumoto folded his hands on the table and began to speak. "As Stacy-*san* may have told you, *Ghost Warriors* is very controversial here in Japan. It is a retelling of one of our most famous historical events. The Forty-Seven Ronin were real samurai who exacted vengeance on Kira, an evil nobleman, for forcing their leader to die a shameful death. They plotted for a year, waiting until they saw the perfect moment to strike against him. Although they eventually killed Kira, they all died in battle. It is an old, beloved story of samurai honor and courage."

"Why does that make *Ghost Warriors* so controversial?" I asked.

"In the books, I have updated the story," Mr. Matsumoto explained. "My samurai do not look or dress like traditional samurai. I've added some unusual touches to their costumes, such as power-enhancing amulets and teleportation devices. But the biggest alteration is that they can become evil, and turn against their old friends. Some feel that dishonors the memory of the real Forty-Seven Ronin."

I nodded. "The big mystery for your contest is how to stop Oishi from going to the dark side. Do you think it could be a disgruntled Forty-Seven Ronin fan who vandalized your office?" I asked.

"Perhaps. The police are going to study the footage from our security cameras. But I have already watched it," Mr. Matsumoto added. "No one came through the lobby."

"The lobby? Don't you have cameras here in the studio itself?" my dad asked.

"No. I thought it would make creative people uncomfortable," he explained. "But let's talk about why you're here, Carson-*san*."

My dad nodded. "I have an appointment with Ken McCarthy this afternoon," he said. "As you know, we went to college together for a couple of years. I hope he'll give me a fair hearing."

Mr. Matsumoto's face hardened. His eyes grew steely, his jaw set. His balled his hands on the table and I could almost feel his anger radiating from him like heat.

"Kenji never gave *me* a fair hearing," he said. "There is so much bad blood between us, Drew-*san*. So much." He stared down at his tea. "It's like the story of the ghost warriors themselves— as if he has turned evil, and has been waiting for years to bring about my downfall. And I have done nothing to deserve it."

Now that there was a real-life mystery to be solved—who trashed Matsumoto Studios?—

George, Bess, and my dad weren't at all surprised when I asked to go with him to Kenji McCarthy's sword making foundry instead of on our whirlwind marathon tourist excursion.

"He may wish to speak to me privately," my dad warned me once we were back in the limo and on our way to see Mr. McCarthy.

"No problem," I said, patting my satchel. "I brought reading material." I pulled out a soft-bound book titled *A History of Japanese Sword Making*. "Did you know that Kenji McCarthy's family has been making swords in Japan since the sixteenth century? Their family name is Sanno, and the Emperor gave them a special crest in 1603. It's their company logo now, and they stamp it on all their sword hilts."

My dad laughed. "Nancy, you may know more about this case than I do. Special crest?"

I flipped open the book and showed him the Sanno crest, which was a dagger surrounded by clouds. "It says there was a terrible fire a few years ago," I continued. "It nearly destroyed the foundry. But Kenji McCarthy single-handedly brought the company back from the ashes. Now Sanno swords are considered the best Japanese swords in the world. Collectors pay thousands of dollars for them."

"I knew he made a lot of money from the company," he said aloud, "which is why it's so unusual that he would sue Mr. Matsumoto over *Ghost Warriors* now."

Our limo was waved through a tall wooden gate by a man in a guard shack, coming into the courtyard of a sprawling, old-fashioned–looking Japanese structure of simple wooden beams and a curved clay tile roof.

A beautiful wooden sign bearing Japanese characters and the words SANNO SWORDS sat in an oval rock garden in front of an open door. Standing in the entrance, a man in an indigo kimono and a pair of raised Japanese sandals bowed, obviously waiting for us.

"Ken," my dad said, getting out of the car and shaking his hand. "It's been so long."

"But you haven't changed a bit," Mr. McCarthy said, with a typical American midwestern accent. He smiled brightly at me. "This can't be your daughter, Nancy. I thought she'd be . . ." He held out his hand to indicate the height of someone half my size. He was wearing a ring with his family crest on his little finger, and I noticed that it was bent at the first knuckle.

"I have a nephew a few years older than you." He sounded very wistful, and I wondered if his nephew lived back in the States. My dad had told me that Kenji McCarthy wasn't very close to the rest of his family, who all lived in the US. He was the only McCarthy who resided in Japan.

"I hope you don't mind that I came along, Mr. McCarthy," I said. I showed him my copy of *A History of Japanese Sword Making*. "I was hoping I could look around your foundry and see how you make swords." And look for evidence that would tie you to the attack on Matsumoto Studios, I added silently.

"It would be a pleasure," he said. "I'll ask one of my employees to show you around."

My dad spent a couple of hours talking to Mr. McCarthy while I got a crash course in making swords. It was fascinating, but my tour guide whisked me through so fast that I didn't have any time to do any detective work.

After my dad and I left, a fog began to roll in, and I found myself thinking of the Ghost Warriors again. Had *I* had a dream about Oishi?

"Did you know that Kenji McCarthy had a dream about Ghost Warriors when he was sixteen?" my dad mused. "That's how he came to create them. He believes that the dream means he is the true owner of the concept."

"Do you believe him?" I asked.

"I've asked to see his original drawings and sketches. Then we'll see."

My dad had plans for dinner with Ichiro Matsumoto to deliver the bad news that Kenji McCarthy still intended to sue him. Bess and George were out shopping, so we organized a place to meet for dinner via cell phone. During our morning limo ride, we had noticed a Spanish-themed restaurant called Fandango located midway between our hotel and Matsumoto Studios. It was close enough to walk to. Although my dad made sure the hotel gave me the best directions on the planet, as well as giving me his number, the hotel's number, and the police number to call if I got lost, he *still* insisted I catch a ride with him in the limo.

The streets were foggy, and as Bess, George, and I sat down at a window table in Fandango, we could barely make out the shapes of pedestrians as they walked down the street. Fandango was filled with young people laughing and eating while Spanish guitar music played in the background. The menus were in Japanese, Spanish, and English, and there were photographs of all the delectable dishes, as well as plastic replicas in the window. I told Bess and George about my trip to the sword factory as we studied the menus.

"They soften the metal and fold it hundreds of times to make a blade. And they stamp the hilt of every sword they make with the Sanno family crest. Mr. McCarthy gave me this." I showed them a key chain, which bore a dagger in the clouds, the symbol of the company known the world over as one of the finest makers of swords.

"Cool," George said. "If I'd known there was going to be a tour, I would have come!"

Bess grinned. "Now let us show you what we bought. I'll go first." She whipped out a bunch of brightly colored, stylish clothes.

George showed me what she'd bought too: a small, rectangular device that looked like a text messenger. She typed in FANDANGO and the street address and pressed a button. Instantly a map popped up in the faceplate.

"Go left. Walk twenty meters," it said in perfect English.

"I programmed it to always take us back to the Sakura Hotel," she said proudly. "We can't get lost!"

"Not that we ever could get lost," Bess added. "The cab drivers here are amazing. All we had to do is show them the addresses of the places we wanted to go, and they took us straight there."

"That is so cool," I said.

"And look at this," Bess said. As she leaned down to pick up her shopping bag, someone brushed past our table and hurried toward the exit. It was Taro Hayashi, carrying a backpack.

"Taro," I called out, and although he didn't appear to hear me, he quickened his pace. As he did so, something fluttered out of his pack.

I bent down and picked it up. "Taro," I called out, "you dropped this." It was noisy in the restaurant, but I figured he still should be able to hear me. "Wait!"

He threw open the door and nearly ran over a couple entering the restaurant. It was a sketch of Oishi, looking much eviler than before, brandishing his samurai sword. There was something familiar about the sword that I couldn't quite place. And then I remembered. I reached in my pocket for the key chain and compared it to Taro's drawing. On the hilt of the sword, Taro had drawn the Sanno family crest.

"I'm going to try to catch up with him," I told Bess and George. "I'll be right back. If the waiter comes, order me some paella."

"Take my GPS thingie," George said, handing it to me.

I took it and scooted out the front door. The

fog was very dense, and the lights of the passing cars bobbed like illuminated balloons as I jogged down the sidewalk with the sketch.

"Taro!" I shouted.

His hunched shoulders and rapid pace signaled urgency, and now I *knew* he was avoiding me. I recognized the landmarks on the streets as he rounded a corner, then crossed the street and jogged down three blocks. We were heading for Matsumoto Studios.

Then he bounded to the curb, hailed a cab, jumped in, and zoomed off.

I was torn between feeling silly—maybe he thought I was following him because I was a crazy fan—and intrigued. He'd acted so strangely today, so . . . *guilty*. And it was awfully strange that he had drawn the crest of the man who was threatening to sue his boss on Oishi's sword. . . .

Maybe it's just a coincidence, I thought. But what if he dropped this sketch on purpose? He might have been trying to get my attention.

I decided to walk the few remaining blocks to the studio. While I walked, I called George on my cell and told her about Taro's drawing and that I was headed to Matsumoto Studios.

I reached Matsumoto Studios in no time, and through the thick fog, I saw Yuki Z. inside the lobby. She opened the door, darted outside, and quickly shut it. She rattled it as if to assure herself that it was locked, and then she started trotting along the side of the building, into a dark alley.

I followed her. She was muttering to herself as she rummaged in a little shoulder-strap purse decorated with the *Ghost Warriors* logo. Maybe she was looking for her cell phone or a bus token. But her head was down, so she didn't see what I saw.

At the opposite end of the alley, three figures seemed to take shape out of the swirling fog. They were dressed in full samurai armor that gleamed in the moonlight, large plates of metal banded together across wide chests and large, powerful arms. They wore long, curving samurai swords at their waists, overskirts of metal, and metal shin guards and big metal shoes. Two large horn shapes protruded from the crowns of their hoodlike helmets, and behind their scowling face guards, the skin on their faces glowed a ghastly, pale white. As I stared at them, circles of light beamed from discs attached to their shoulders.

Ghost Warriors.

"Yuki," I said softly. She didn't hear me as she continued to search through her purse. Finally she huffed and zipped it closed. When she raised her head, she saw the three menacing figures, staring straight at us. She froze, covering her mouth. She began to walk backward toward me.

"Yuki," I said more loudly.

"Nancy-*san*." Her voice was shaking. She glanced at me, but kept her attention fixed on the three samurai. They pulled out their swords and began walking toward us through the fog. I could hear the clanking of their heavy shoes on the pavement. A dozen thoughts raced through my mind—not real ghosts, publicity stunt—and I tried to make myself move to go into the lobby. But I couldn't.

I'm scared, I thought. Too scared to move!

Yuki screamed and headed straight for me. She grabbed my wrist and dragged me toward the front entrance of the building just as a security guard opened the door.

She spoke to him in Japanese and he leaped into action, rushing outside. We hurried inside and Yuki slammed the door shut. The guard was back in less than ten seconds, a cell phone pressed against his ear. He said something to Yuki in Japanese.

"Nancy-*san*," Yuki murmured, "no one was in the alley. They disappeared!"

"Is he calling the police?" I asked.

"He will. But first he is calling Mr. Matsumoto," Yuki explained. "Is your father still with him?"

"I don't know." I used my own cell phone to call George and Bess, who were freaking out because I'd been gone so long. They promised to stay at the restaurant until I could get there. Then I called my dad and told him what had happened.

"Nancy, stay there." He sounded very worried. "I'll come and get you."

"We can take a taxi," Yuki said. "I'll drop you and your friends at the hotel, then I will go home." I told my dad the plan, but he didn't like the sound of it.

"Dad, we're less than ten minutes away from the hotel. Yuki will be with us. I can handle it," I said gently. I didn't suppose it would ease his mind to remind him that I had been in far worse situations before.

The cab arrived. Yuki and I picked up Bess and George, who had had my paella boxed up, and the cab drove through the foggy streets back toward our hotel. Bess and George asked a hundred questions about what had happened, and Yuki learned very quickly that I had wound up at Matsumoto Studios because I was following

Taro Hayashi. When I showed Yuki the sketch, her eyes widened and she got very quiet.

We reached the hotel, and George and Bess slid out. Yuki held out her arm to stop me from getting out.

"Nancy, please, do not tell Mr. Matsumoto about Taro," she said, her eyes searching mine. "About that sketch."

"Isn't it strange that Taro drew the Sanno logo on Oishi's sword," I said, pointing at the sketch, "given that Ken McCarthy, the owner of Sanno Swords, is threatening to sue Matsumoto Studios."

She reached for the sketch. I let her take it.

"Sanno is the most famous swordmaker in Japan," she said. "Taro is an artist. He doesn't think of the problem between Mr. Matsumoto and Kenji McCarthy."

She sure was being defensive of Taro. And then it dawned on me. "He's your boyfriend." I said out loud.

She blinked. "My . . . yes," she blurted. "Yes, he is, and Mr. Matsumoto would be so angry. So, please say nothing."

"Please," she repeated.

"Okay, I won't. For now," I emphasized. First, I was going to do a little investigating. Yuki and Taro may have been dating in secret, but that still didn't explain his sketch, or the way he'd acted in the restaurant.

"Thank you." She dipped her head. "*Oyasumi-nasai*. Good night, Nancy-*san*."

"Good night," I said.

George, Bess, and I discussed the situation while I ate my paella.

"So Taro freaked out and left the restaurant because he's dating Yuki?" Bess asked.

"And then there's the sketch," I added. "A sketch that could make his boss very angry."

"Right after a break-in," George added.

I thought a minute. "Maybe the break-in was a publicity stunt that Yuki staged," I said. "And Taro was in on it. Then it went bad, and they were meeting at Fandango to do damage control."

"Sounds good," Bess said.

"But then what about tonight? It didn't feel like a publicity stunt, and those figures didn't look like actors." I shivered, remembering the three ghostly forms in the alley.

Bess shook her head. "I would have fainted dead away."

By the time my dad returned to the hotel, he was more upset than I had seen him in a long time. I went to his room, where we talked over my suspicions, and I told him about the sketch.

"That wasn't too bright of Taro Hayahsi," he said, wincing. "Drawing a Sanno sword when his employer is having problems with Kenji. But Sanno swords *are* world famous."

"But then why did he run out of the restaurant if he had nothing to hide?" I asked my dad.

He frowned. "And as angry as Mr. Matsumoto was, he refused to call the police. He said something about that not being the Japanese way. I didn't understand it. I still don't. There were police there yesterday."

"I'll move around the puzzle pieces," I said, "and see if I can come up with anything."

"You do that, girl detective," he said, smiling at me. "So long as you're *careful*."

I kissed him good night and returned to my room. George and Bess were both asleep. Then the hotel room phone rang and I grabbed it.

"Nancy-*san*?" It was Taro. "I need to speak to you as soon as possible."

"Okay," I ventured, whispering so as not to wake my cousins.

"In person. Please." He sounded very frightened.

I had a funny sensation; it was almost as if I could *feel* my brain moving several random pieces of the puzzle: his crooked finger; the Sanno crest

33

on Oishi's sword; and Ken McCarthy's crooked finger.

"Taro," I said slowly, "you're Kenji McCarthy's nephew."

There was a long pause. "Please, let us meet in person," he said. "There is a large koi pond on the grounds of the Sakura. *Please*."

"Okay," I said. "You and me. Maybe Yuki. Nobody else. No Ghost Warriors."

"Yuki and I will be there," he promised.

Half an hour later, I paced alone beside the beautiful koi pond, although it was so foggy it reminded me more of a swamp in a horror movie. Through the layers of mist I could see enormous orange and gold fish swimming around. A breeze cleared the surface and I tensed, half-expecting to see a ghostly face staring back at me.

I heard footsteps and turned around to see Taro and Yuki walking anxiously toward me.

I bowed. They bowed back.

"Thank you for giving that drawing to Yuki," he began.

"You're welcome," I replied. Then I waited.

Taro took a deep breath. "You're right," he said, lifting his gaze toward mine. "My real name is Hideo Sanno, and I'm Kenji McCarthy's nephew."

"Now you have solved one mystery," Yuki told me.

Yuki and I huddled in our jackets beside the pond as Hideo Sanno paced, his story spilling out of him.

"My parents are both dead," he explained, "and I was raised by friends of theirs. But I visited Uncle Kenji often. He is Japanese-American, but he has lived in Japan for most of his life. He loves old, traditional things. He's not a very modern person at all."

He stopped for a moment.

"Is something wrong?" I asked him.

"I thought I saw someone across the pond," he said. "It was just my imagination."

"Someone . . . ?" I asked, looking in the same direction as he.

"It's nothing." He looked away. "Where was I? When I was finishing high school, I found his old Ghost Warrior sketches and drawings, and I told him I wanted to become an artist, just like him. He said it was a terrible idea. He said art would break my heart. After a while, I stopped going to see him, because he was so bitter, and he didn't support what I wanted to do with my life.

"I was hanging my work in a friend's gallery in Roppongi one day when one of Matsumoto-*san*'s executives walked in off the street. He told me he would like to show some of my pieces to Matsumoto-*san*. I knew the story of the hatred between them, so I lied to him and told him my name was Taro Hayashi. I was hired."

"I found out by accident," Yuki said. "I promised I would keep his secret. Mr. Matsumoto would fire me if he knew I kept such a secret."

Taro—Hideo—ran his hands through his hair. "Nancy-*san*, I saw Uncle Kenji's original drawings. They are very different from the *Ghost Warriors* of today. Very old-style. Not popular."

"So Mr. Matsumoto made a lot of changes," I said.

"He's a genius," he replied, his dark eyes shining. "Working for him is my dream. I've learned so much. But if he finds out who I am . . ." He made a face.

"Maybe you could go to him," I said, "and explain everything."

"What if Matsumoto-*san* asks me to testify against my uncle?" he said. "I could never do that. My loyalty is torn in two."

"But *you* didn't vandalize the office for your uncle," I said, knowing it was true.

He shook his head. "No. But Mr. Matsumoto will never believe me if he finds out who I am."

"And you?" I asked Yuki. "Please, Yuki, tell me the truth."

"I didn't," she said emphatically. "It is the ghosts. The Ghost Warriors are real!" She frowned at Taro. "You don't believe me, but I have seen them before. I thought I saw Oishi once, staring at me through the window."

I felt a little chill run down my spine. "I think I may have seen him once too," I admitted.

The three of us stared at one another. "My uncle said he dreamed of the Ghost Warriors when he was sixteen," Hideo said in a low, hushed voice. "He also believes they're real. I thought he was crazy."

"Oishi-*san*, we will make everything good," Yuki said, bowing low into the fog.

Ripples formed in the fish pond. The wind caught my hair; something touched my cheek. I jerked and saw a crinkled brown leaf, dancing in the night breeze. But it had felt more like fingertips. . . .

"Oishi-*san* wants us to solve this mystery," Yuki insisted. "You and me, Nancy-*san*."

"And me as well," Hideo said.

"Then we will," I promised them both.

We three bowed, and they walked across the misty grounds toward the street. I scanned left and right as I headed back toward the lobby, just as the doors whirled open and my two cousins trotted out, fully dressed.

"What are you doing?" I asked them.

"We could ask the same thing, but we know you too well to even bother," Bess said. "I woke up and saw you weren't in bed, and your big purse was gone. So I figured you'd gone out sleuthing, and I woke up George. We weren't going to let you sneak around Tokyo without us."

"We saw you talking to Taro and Yuki," George added.

I filled them in on the rest of the story.

"You felt as if someone had touched your cheek?" Bess replied. "Are you sure?"

"It was a leaf," I said, not very convincingly. "Okay, let's go back to Matsumoto Studios and see if we can find any evidence to explain who sent those Ghost Warriors," I suggested.

George made a face. "Because the first time you saw them in the alley wasn't scary enough?"

"It's not the fear factor that's driving me, it's the clue factor," I reminded them both.

"Your dad reminded us to be careful," George said.

"If my dad finds out, I'll take the blame," I assured her. "And we'll go on foot, and use the map-o-matic if we need directions."

"We may as well," Bess ventured. "For sure I'm not going to be able to sleep."

Although it was cold, we decided we'd be safer walking the short distance to Matsumoto Studios rather than taking a cab. The fog had rolled in, obscuring the street, the cars, and the moon. We used George's fancy new mapping system to find our way. It was like being blind. I wondered if there was any point to our excursion, but I'm like a bloodhound when it comes to looking for clues, and I didn't want to miss my chance.

"*Turn right,*" the map ordered us.

I led the cousins around the block so that we entered the alley at the end where the ghost warriors had stood, and shone my flashlight over the curtains of fog. My heart was thundering.

"This isn't going to work," Bess said.

I knew she was right. We didn't have enough visual range to see our feet, much less any clues. I was just about to suggest we go back to the hotel, when I stepped on something hard and flat. I dropped down and aimed my flashlight at it. It was like peering through murky water. I put it in my purse and moved forward, feeling for other objects.

Then, suddenly, I was certain that someone was nearby, observing us. The hair on the back of my neck stood straight up and my hands were trembling.

"This is scary. Let's get out of here," Bess begged.

We half ran, half walked as the wind whipped up. When we got back to the lobby of the Sakura, I pulled the object out of my purse. It was a sword hilt stamped with the Sanno crest. Mr. McCarthy's crest.

"Uh-oh," George said, gazing at me.

In the morning, I found a note under our door.

Hi, Nancy,

Golfing with Ichiro and his legal team. Then I'll be in meetings, then another business dinner. Be careful. If you decide to go sightseeing, take taxis and don't go far. Stick to public areas. And please be back well before dark.

Love,

Dad

PS: Please check in with me on my cell.

I showed the note to George and Bess. "We're on our own," I told them.

"So, what are we going to do?" Bess asked.

"I think I'm going to see if I can visit Kenji McCarthy," I replied. Before they could say anything, I added, "I think he's more likely to talk to me if I'm alone."

"Hey," George said, looking up the interactive Tokyo map on her laptop. "The shrine where the Forty-Seven Ronin are buried is here in Tokyo. Bess, you want to go check it out?"

Bess was all for it. The hotel offered a tour to the temple on a bus, so they gave me the electronic map. My friends went off to sightsee, and I went to see a man about a sword hilt.

When I called Mr. McCarthy to ask if I might come by, he said that would be fine and talked to the hotel desk so they could give my taxi directions.

"It's nice to see you again," he began as he led me into a small, traditionally decorated Japanese room with a woven straw floor, a simple wood table, and cushions for us to sit on. "You said you had some more questions about sword making."

"Yes. I was wondering what kind of sword this came from," I said, as I pulled the hilt from my satchel and put it on the table.

He sucked in his breath. Then he gingerly picked it up and turned it over, examining it.

"This hilt is at least thirty years old," he said. "We had to modify the crest because the original stamp was destroyed in the fire. Where did you get it?"

"I think a Ghost Warrior dropped it last night," I told him. Then I described the scene in the alley, leaving out the part about Hideo.

He muttered something under his breath, then led me over to a computer. "I don't know if this will show up," he said. "I hired a firm to do an inventory of everything we owned after the fire. Each of our hilts is numbered, because all our swords are handmade, one-of-a-kind." He pointed to some tiny numerals beneath the logo.

He poised his fingers over the keyboard, then stopped. "Wait. Ichiro and I made some Ghost Warrior costumes so we could show investors our concept. Ichiro got the fabric and I provided the swords. I forgot about that."

I blinked. "So . . . is it possible he had possession of this hilt?"

He nodded, looking sour and angry. "Yes, it is possible. Possible that he trashed his own offices and tried to put the blame on me. Yes, your father mentioned that when he came to see me. I told him it was more likely an employee was angry with Ichiro for stealing his work and saying it was his."

He reached for the phone on his desk. "I'm calling my lawyer and telling him to move forward with the lawsuit," he said angrily.

"Please, wait," I said. "Let me see if I can . . . do something about all this. Please."

Scowling, he took the hilt from me. "Your father is working for Ichiro. Why should I trust you?"

"He's not working for him. He's here unofficially, for his friend in Hollywood, trying to see if you two can settle out of court."

"We can't," he said, and his pain and anger made his face look . . . Oishi-like. I shivered.

"Thank you for seeing me," I said, and then I left.

I knew I didn't have all the puzzle pieces yet, but I did have some, and I thought it was time to tell my dad about them. I called him on his cell phone, but my call wouldn't go through.

I called the studio and spoke to Yuki, asking if she and/or Hideo could sneak me into the studio after closing.

"Why?" she whispered.

"I have a theory about who vandalized the studio," I said, "and I think the proof is in the office."

Hideo got on her phone. "I'll do whatever I can to help *Ghost Warriors*," he said in a low, hushed voice.

I wondered if I should tell him *who* I thought had trashed the studio. I thought about the Ghost Warriors and their leader, Oishi. Would the Ghost Warriors follow Oishi if they discovered he'd become evil? Or would they turn against him?

Shortly after lunch, George and Bess returned from the shrine of the Forty-Seven Ronin, very excited and eager to tell me all about it.

"They moved through the fog when they attacked," George said. "Their enemies never saw them until it was too late!"

That was on my mind when Hideo met me around the corner from the studio with a large, wheeled crate that reminded me of a coffin. He had cushioned it with packing material, and after I climbed in, he arranged a layer of souvenir bobblehead Ghost Warriors on top of me.

Then he wheeled me into the main entrance. The bobbleheads chattered like those little toy windup false teeth. He paused and spoke to some-one in Japanese—I assumed it was the security guard—and then he pushed me across the lobby and into the elevator. I heard the door close.

We headed up. "So far, it's good," he whis-pered.

I heard the doors open, and then he wheeled me out to an inconspicuous spot. Then I waited for what seemed like forever.

I had a bad cramp in my foot by the time I felt the vibration of footfalls and the lifting of the crate lid. The tray of bobbleheads was removed, and then Hideo helped me out.

"Okay," he said. "What do you want me to do?"

I knew he was taking a big risk sneaking me in. I didn't want him to get in trouble. So I said, "Just watch for the elevator. If it starts to move, come and warn me."

"All right," he said. "Here's the key to Mr. Matsumoto's office."

Yuki had come through—she knew that there was an extra key to his office with the downstairs security guard, and she had palmed it on her way back from lunch.

Hideo tiptoed to the elevator to stand guard. I didn't dare turn on the lights. But any good detective carries a flashlight with her, even in

Tokyo, so I turned on my tiny but very bright pencil light and, cupping it, began going through the brushed steel drawers of his high-tech desk. Nothing. I opened up his file cabinets. Nothing there, either.

I checked the time. I had already been there for half an hour! I moved to a small closet containing a bag of golf clubs and a raincoat. And a zipped-up garment bag.

Golf clubs? I thought. He went to play golf with my dad this morning!

I went back to the golf bag and peered inside.

Bingo. The bag was filled with swords.

I grabbed up the first one and carefully pulled it out. I saw the ripples where the metal had been folded and refolded so many times. I noted the hilt, which had the same kind of older-style hilt as the one I had shown Mr. McCarthy. There was a second sword, nearly identical, and a third, minus its hilt.

I took a deep breath and called George, who had traded cell phones with me before I left. Hers was far more high-tech than mine, of course.

"Three swords, two hilts," I said. "I'm taking pictures."

I took several with George's phone, and e-mailed them to George. Then I put the swords back. I returned to the garment bag and unzipped it, hoping to find a Ghost Warriors costume or three.

It was empty. Disappointed, I felt along the sides for a piece of fabric, anything that might prove it had once held samurai costumes. I knelt and patted the bottom . . . and I found what felt like a piece of varnished cardboard.

I pulled it out and shined my flashlight on it. It was an old Polaroid snapshot of a very young Ichiro Matsumoto standing with an equally young Kenji McCarthy, with their arms around a third man in full samurai battle armor. The costumes I had seen the night before were a lot more fanciful, but I put the picture in my purse anyway.

The phone vibrated. "Nancy, you've got some evidence," George told me. "Let's wrap this up."

"Okay," I said. "It's Bess's turn."

That was Bess's cue to create a diversion. She was supposed to walk over to the main door of the building and flirt with the security guard, asking him in English if he could help her find her way back to the Sakura. Bess was fashion-model gorgeous, and she had used her natural flirting skills to help me solve cases before.

I called Bess.

"Here we go," she told me. She kept her cell

phone on, and I heard her humming as she crossed the street. "Yoo-hoo! Good evening!" she called to the guard, rapping on the door. "Do you remember me? Can you help me?"

By then I was standing upstairs next to the elevator with Hideo. I knew he wanted to ask me if I'd found anything, but I pressed my finger against my lips, cautioning silence. As Bess's voice faded, I took a chance and pushed the button for the lobby. I also turned off the cell phone. Hideo crossed his fingers. I crossed mine, too.

The elevator descended; I held my breath when the door slid open. Then I grinned at Hideo. The security guard's desk was vacant and the front door was wide open. I set down the key and we ran on the balls of our feet to the open door, peering through the glass to see where Bess had led the man. They were all the way across the street with their backs to the entrance, and he was pointing in the direction of the hotel.

We slipped out and darted into the alley. Yuki was there, waiting to see how it went. Shielded by the shadows, I dialed Bess's phone to let her know that the coast was clear.

"Did you find anything?" Hideo asked me.

"I think I did, but I want to make sure before I say anything," I told him.

****

Once the guard was back inside, we snuck across the street and hustled back to the hotel. Hideo and Yuki said good night there. I tried to call my dad, but the call still wouldn't connect. So the three of us decided to wait up for him.

Then, about what happened next . . . well, I keep telling myself I must have fallen asleep and dreamed the whole thing. But I distinctly remember walking to the window and gazing out at the fog. I murmured, "Oishi-*san*?"

The fog swirled and danced, and I took an uncertain step back. I was almost positive I could see a face in the fog, but there were no glowing red eyes. It was a blur, and I told myself I was making myself see a face there, when there really wasn't one.

But as I turned away, I heard a voice.

"Ask him about the fire." It was low and breathy, and it was one of the most frightening things I have ever heard in my life.

The next thing I knew, my dad was shaking me gently. He looked very somber and he said, "George showed me the pictures you took last night. Nancy, why didn't you tell me what you were doing?"

"I'm sorry," I said. "It was all happening so fast."

"I'm meeting Ichiro at ten this morning," he said, "and I want you to be there. I want you to bring the pictures on both the laptop and George's phone."

"Okay, Dad," I said. I hoped I hadn't ruined things for him. Or for anyone else.

I thought we would be going to Matsumoto Studios, but instead we went to Sengaku-ji, the temple where the Forty-Seven Ronin were buried. The fog was thick as we walked beneath several large, red, wooden gates topped with sloping tile roofs.

"Why did we come here?" I asked him.

"Ichiro told me that he and Ken came here when they became partners," my dad said. "It's a place haunted by memories of happier times between them. I thought it might make this conversation go a little more smoothly."

I knew he was focusing on the word "happier," but I was stuck on "haunted." We walked to the grave sites of the Forty-Seven Ronin, which were long stone rectangles with Japanese characters carved on them. There was a statue of their leader, Oishi, who didn't look a thing like his manga version. Fresh flowers sat in vases at all the graves, but whoever put them there was gone. We were alone, just my dad and I, with George's phone and laptop.

Mr. Matsumoto showed up, smiling and pleasant.

"A nice gesture, Carson-*san*," he said, "to come for a visit together at the temple of the original Ghost Warriors." I noticed they were on a first-name basis, and I wondered if this was going to be hard for my dad.

"I have something to talk to you about," my dad began. He cleared his throat. "I brought my daughter along with me because she's been doing a little detective work on her own. I didn't know, I assure you, but now that she has brought certain things to my attention, I think we need to discuss them."

Mr. Matsumoto frowned at my dad and then at me. Then my dad opened George's laptop and turned it on. The picture I had taken of the swords came up, and Mr. Matsumoto's mouth dropped open.

"I'm sorry," I said. "I went into your office, and I found them in your golf bag. One of them is missing the hilt. I found it in the alley by the studio."

He lowered his head. All the fight seemed to

leave him. "It was such a stupid thing to do. I knew it was stupid, and I still did it."

"Were you going to claim that Ken was harassing you by breaking into your studio and frightening your employees?" my dad asked. "To try to influence the court?"

Sighing heavily, Mr. Matsumoto nodded. "I hired the actors to appear in the alley last night because I knew Yuki was working late. She's so impressionable."

"Which is why you didn't want to call the police," I guessed.

"Yes, young detective."

"What about the security guard?"

"I told him to stay with your two girls. That gave my actors the time they needed. I feel terrible," he whispered.

"And you vandalized your own office?"

"To make Kenji look bad," he confessed. "I was so angry at him. So afraid that he would ruin everything if he sued me. After all my hard work . . ."

"But why didn't you get rid of the evidence?" I asked him. "Those sword hilts are one of a kind. That makes them easy to trace."

"I couldn't make myself let go of the proof that once, he was my friend," Mr. Matsumoto replied, sighing heavily. "Carson-*san*, I can no longer expect you to help me. I'm disgraced."

He plopped onto a stone bench and hung his head. I had rarely seen a man look so defeated. Then I remembered my strange dream, or vision, or ghostly visitation—whatever it was.

"What about the fire?" I asked.

In an instant, the humbled, embarrassed man jumped to his feet. His face contorted with anger, all trace of humiliation gone.

"That fire!" he shouted. I took a step back. "I'm not surprised you've heard about it. Kenji spread rumors all over Japan. Well, let me tell you exactly what happened."

"Please do," I said.

"Kenji came to me with the idea for *Ghost Warriors*. He wanted to tell the story of the Forty-Seven Ronin in a very traditional way. I thought we should try to update it. We fought constantly. We were truly like two colliding warlords, and our friendship was in tatters. And to make things worse, we couldn't sell *Ghost Warriors* to anyone. No one liked it.

"It was such a struggle. I was working by day as a computer programmer, and Kenji was trying to keep Sanno Swords alive. But he had no money, and workmanship at the foundry was poor. He could barely keep the company going."

"So both of you were very stressed," I said. "You probably fought even more because of that."

"That's very perceptive of you," Mr. Matsumoto replied. His voice dropped. "Then there was that terrible fire at the foundry, and it burned to the ground. His family back in America had no interest in rebuilding. They told Kenji there was no market for traditional Japanese swords, and he was on his own."

Mr. Matsumoto fell silent for a moment, as if he were seeing the past unfold before him.

"I had recently inherited some money, and my first thought was that I could quit my hated job. Instead, I went to Kenji and offered to buy his half of the rights to *Ghost Warriors*. I reminded him that he would have no say in it and he would make no money from it. He agreed. He said *Ghost Warriors* was a failure and that he didn't care what happened to it."

He paced back and forth. "After I gave him the money, I was penniless. I knew then that I had to make *Ghost Warriors* succeed. I had nothing else. I stayed up night after night, eating ramen, watching Kenji rebuild his foundry. Now that he had some capital, and could make some improvements, he became a true artisan. His swords made him very rich. While *I* was deeply in debt, with a concept no one wanted."

I pulled the Polaroid from my satchel and looked at the two smiling young men. Ichiro and Kenji, in happier times?

Around the corner, a flicker of movement made me jump nearly out of my skin. But it was no ghost walking toward us from among the tombstones. It was Kenji McCarthy. I raised my hand in greeting. But it was almost as if someone put my hand down and pressed a ghostly finger to my lips, telling me to stay silent.

"I was willing to do anything," Mr. Matsumoto said, unaware that Mr. McCarthy stood close by, listening. "I threw away our original concept and started over so many times. I totally redesigned our look—I not only updated it, but I made it cutting-edge. Crazy, wild, and different. Then it finally happened. . . . I got a deal. A great deal. I couldn't believe it."

He took a deep breath. "I was going to tell Kenji I wanted to give him some of the money. I spent weeks making sure the amount I was offering him would be fair—I had given my inheritance, and I had worked for years with no pay. But I knew that without Kenji, there would have been no *Ghost Warriors*."

"So what happened?" I asked, glancing over at Mr. McCarthy. He was wearing a pained expression as he gazed at his one-time friend.

Mr. Matsumoto looked off in the distance, as if at the past; his face became harsh and almost crazed with anger, like Oishi when he was turning evil.

"*Kenji* came to *me* first. He said I must have made the deal *before* the fire. Then he said that I set the fire myself, so he would agree to sell his half of *Ghost Warriors* to me!"

I inhaled sharply. What a terrible accusation. Glancing back at Mr. McCarthy hiding behind the tombstones, I opened my mouth to say something, but again, I felt something urging me to stay silent. My dad was quiet too, and I wasn't sure if he knew that Mr. McCarthy was there.

"That accusation haunted me for years. To this day, there are businessmen who will not deal with me, because they heard about what Kenji said. It wounded me so deeply. It cut my soul."

"I can understand that," I said quietly.

He clenched his fists. "And still, when Ms. Stacy contacted me, I thought of going to Kenji and offering him some of the money she was offering. But as usual, he came to me first, demanding half the profits, half of every dime I ever made from *Ghost Warriors*, or he would sue me. And that's where you came in, Drew-*san*," he said to my dad.

A wind whipped up. Leaves danced in a circle around the tombstone, then settled in a pile at Kenji McCarthy's feet.

He stepped from the shadows.

"I am so ashamed," he said. Tears were welling in his eyes. "Ichiro, forgive me. I . . . I never heard your side of this. I can see how badly I behaved. I don't even know what to say."

The two men faced each other, standing in the temple of the Forty-Seven Ronin. Fog rolled in on the wind, and I shivered. I looked to my left, and I thought I saw a figure watching. Then the wind blew again, revealing only mist.

"Kenji?" Mr. Matsumoto croaked, barely able to get out the word. "I did not start that fire. And I would never knowingly profit from the misfortune of another."

"Ichiro, I've been so wrong . . . so ungrateful . . ."

The two warlords stared at each other. Then they slowly walked past the graves of the Forty-Seven Ronin, stopped, and bowed deeply to each other. I guessed it was the samurai way of saying they were sorry.

★★★★

On the last night of our trip to Japan, Matsumoto-*san* and McCarthy-*san* took my dad, Bess, George, Hideo, Yuki, and me out for dinner in a fancy restaurant overlooking a beautiful Japanese garden. Hideo had confessed who he was to both of them, and they laughed their heads off, agreeing that the audacious kid was the way they had been, back in the day.

While everyone was eating and chatting, Kenji McCarthy asked to speak with me. As it was a surprisingly warm evening, we agreed to walk in the garden. We wound our way over a little stone bridge surrounded by artfully arranged rocks and trimmed trees, and gazed down at some koi in a pond that was much larger than the one at our hotel. The large, white moon cast a silver sheen over the landscape, making it glow.

"I wanted to thank you for saving me," he said. "Not because you told me what Ichiro was doing, which *was* stupid." He chuckled. "You made me see how badly I had treated him. I can't believe I ever thought such terrible things about a man who tried so hard to be a good friend."

"The past is the past," I said.

"I was haunted by it. We *were* two warlords colliding, and my jealousy and anger *had* turned me evil. But now . . . we have a chance again."

My dad had already told Janelle Stacy that Kenji McCarthy was dropping his lawsuit. She was ecstatic, of course. We were going to stop in Los Angeles on our way home to do some serious celebrating.

"Do you think you'll work together on *Ghost Warriors* again?" I asked.

He shrugged. "I dreamed up the original idea, but he did so much more with it. I like old-style Japanese things, like handmade swords. Maybe it's enough that Hideo's involved."

He cocked his head. "Talking about the fire is what saved us. Having to discuss it once more, face to face. Do you know that Asano, the original master of the Forty-Seven Ronin, died because he answered an insult with a sword blow? He had no way to talk about it. He could only strike back. How did you know to bring up the fire, Nancy?"

I gazed out over the pond. "I think it came to me in a dream, but I can't really be sure. I heard Oishi telling me to ask about the fire. Maybe . . . maybe it was a ghost," I whispered. Mr. McCarthy was the only person I had revealed that to. I hadn't even told my dad.

"I believe that ghosts live in dreams," he said.

"I believe that I dreamed of the Ghost Warriors because they *are* real, and because they wanted their story to be told."

"I believe that too," I replied, and I realized that I really did.

"Domo arigato gozaimashita." He bowed very low, bestowing honor on me. "That means thank you for all you have done for me."

"You're welcome," I said, bowing back.

Then he walked away, and I stood alone, in the fog. Still, I felt someone watching me.

I straightened, lifting my gaze from the koi to some trees. Goose bumps ran up and down my spine as a shimmering white figure across the pond gazed straight at me, and bowed.

I knew it was Oishi. I just knew it.

Or maybe it was just the night mist of Tokyo, telling secrets to the wind.

THE END

america's got terror!

"Help! Zombies are rising from the grave!" my boyfriend Ned called out, laughing as he leaned over the white picket fence surrounding my brand-new fruit and vegetable garden. Hannah Gruen, our housekeeper; our gardening-expert friend, Evangeline Waters; and I had worked all day planting and mulching, and I was tired, hungry . . . and caked with dirt.

"We're not zombies, we're garden gnomes, silly," I informed him, rising to my feet and wiping my face with a clean rag.

"And organic garden gnomes at that," Evangeline added, sprinkling the last bit of mulch around the pumpkins. "No toxic pesticides for these beautiful crops . . . or the people who will eventually eat them."

"That would include me, I hope," Nick said. "Especially if I help weed?"

"It's a deal," I told him. "Since we aren't using

any weed killers, we'll have a lot of weeds to pull."

"We wanted to get the garden in before Nancy goes off ghost busting tomorrow," Evangeline said as we gathered together our gardening trowels, shovels, and rakes.

Hannah shivered. "I still don't like the idea of your going there, Nancy."

I shrugged as I closed up our potato sack of mulch. "It's just a creepy old house."

"A 'creepy old house' that a crazy old lady spent the last twenty-nine years of her life building," Hannah argued. "It's a monstrosity."

"I used to sneak in there with my older sister when we were girls," Evangeline confessed. "She would dare me to go upstairs. Once I got as far as the third stair, but I always lost my nerve. That enormous place just terrified me! When you come back, Nancy, tell me what was up there."

"I will," I promised, placing the sack of mulch in our garden shed. "I have to go make myself presentable," I told Ned. "I'm going to borrow a book from Lucia. Are you coming back for the 'bon voyage' dinner for George, Bess, and me?"

"More like a 'boo voyage' dinner," he quipped. "I'll be here."

★★★★

About an hour later, I entered the Psychic's Parlor on River Street. Spicy incense greeted me as I pushed aside the beaded curtain leading into the exotic "reading" room. River Heights' local psychic, Lucia Gonzalvo, was sitting at the circular table draped in black velvet. Several tarot cards were arranged in a pattern before her. Her fingertips rested on a card featuring a skeleton dressed in armor riding on a horse. Beneath the horse's hooves, DEATH was spelled out in capital letters.

"Nancy, hello," she said in her exotic accent. "I need to talk to you." She gestured to the cards. "I've been getting vibes all day that you should stay away from Hackett Mansion. That there's danger there." Her voice lowered. "That it is truly haunted and the spirit who walks there is troubled."

I was taken aback. "You're not teasing me, are you?"

She gazed down at the cards. "I've always freely admitted that what I do here in the parlor is a little bit show biz and a little bit friendly guidance, but this feels very different. I don't know what it is. It's a mystery to me." Grimacing, she closed her eyes. "That was the wrong word to use, wasn't it?"

I smiled faintly. "Saying 'mystery' to me is kind of like saying 'go!' to a greyhound." I sat across from her at the table and took her hands in mine. "Lucia, Sarah Hackett started building that mansion in 1883 after her husband drowned in the Muskoka River. She didn't stop construction on it until 1912. No one knows why. None of the public has been permitted on the property for decades, and I have a chance to stay there for a week! I already signed all the consent forms and so did George and Bess. How can I say no now?"

She turned my hand over and stared at my palm. Whatever she saw there, it bothered her. Closing her fingers over mine, she sighed heavily, reached down and picked up a large hardback book titled *Murder Mansion: The True Story of the Haunted Hackett House.*

She handed it to me.

"I don't know how," she said, "but I wish you would."

George, Bess, and I had been selected as contestants for a new reality show called *Can You Hack It?* We had to spend an entire week inside Hackett Mansion, unless we got so scared we asked to leave. Kate, the show's casting agent, had "absolutely, one hundred percent" promised us that all the magic of Hollywood would be used for the express purpose of scaring the wits out of us.

"Screams mean ratings," Kate explained.

Once the series aired, the TV audience would get to vote for their favorite "Scream Queen" or "Scream King" among those who made it through the entire week. The winner would win prizes donated by different companies, mostly around a Halloween theme, but the grand prize was a starring role in the next horror movie to be directed by Rafael Elizondo, the same man who was directing *Can You Hack It?*

Tomorrow at six a.m. sharp, a bus would pick us up and drive us to the "extremely haunted" Hackett Mansion (so the show press kit read), way out in the boonies ("too far away for anyone to hear you *scream*!"), on a cliff overlooking the Muskoka River ("where Sarah Hackett's husband, Nathan, *drowned* . . . or did he? Was he *pushed*? Or did he *leap* to his *death*, to escape an *even worse fate*?")

Starstruck Bess was the one who heard about *Can You Hack It?* and encouraged her cousin George, my boyfriend, Ned, and me to apply. I didn't get my hopes up that all of us would be selected. Unfortunately, Ned was turned down because he was "press." He worked part-time for his dad, the owner of the *River Heights Bugle*, our local newspaper.

After dinner, we munched on large slices of Hannah's chocolate cake and cups of soothing chamomile tea. Ned swears milk was created to go with chocolate cake so he had a nice tall glass. While we savored Hannah's kitchen magic, I told them about Lucia's warning.

"Well, I have the creeps times two. But I'm still going," Bess insisted. "This may be my big break! I have got to be the Scream Queen! I'll star in a horror movie!"

"Well, you're not going without me," I told her.

"And I'm not getting left behind," George put in. "So that's *that*. Now, the big question is, do we tell Deirdre? Do we warn her that Lucia says there's big trouble at Hackett Mansion?" Because, of course, our nemesis had been selected for the show too.

"Yes," we all said in unison.

"Because maybe *she'll* listen to reason, and stay home," Bess chirped. Deirdre had always had it in for us—mostly me—and it would be a far more pleasant experience to be scared to death without her around to make it worse.

"You always were an optimist," her cousin chided her.

"Some see the bucket of blood as half empty," Bess retorted. "I prefer to see it half full."

Ned shook his head. "And *I* see I'm going to miss a very interesting week."

"And *I'll* miss *you*," I told him.

We told Deirdre what Lucia had said before we boarded the bus to go to the mansion. But instead of thanking us, she accused us of trying to frighten her out of participating. She may be catty and superficial, but she *isn't* naive.

"I'm going to stay the entire week," she boasted as we bounced along on the reality show's bus. I was still waving good-bye to Ned, who had come to see us off. It took three hours for us to say good-bye seven times, since Rafael, the director, kept urging us to act as if we were afraid we might never see our loved ones again while his two cameras recorded every fake tear and over-dramatic trembling lip.

"They won't get me to leave, no matter how they try to frighten us," Deirdre went on. "I am *so* ready for prime time." She gave her newly highlighted dark hair a toss. "I had a total spa day yesterday"—she wiggled her French manicure—"and then I went shopping for new clothes." She gestured to her red boatneck sweater, red beaded necklace, and matching earrings. "Red looks best on camera, you know."

"Yeah, except then everyone will miss the blood when you die a hideous on-camera death," George drawled.

"That's the exact reason everything I packed is white," Bess said.

She was still staring at the Starbucks coffee I had bought for her, because, she insisted, she was too sleepy to drink it. I wondered if she had really thought through her dream of becoming a movie star. When I had gone to Los Angeles with my dad, the actors we had met were always complaining about how early they had to get up when they were filming.

"You are not funny," Deirdre informed Bess. "Neither are you, George."

"All right, Hackees, let's get back to work," Rafael told us. There were ten of us. Deirdre, Bess, George, twin guys named David and Chard (for "Richard"), and I were the contestants from River Heights. The others were a bouncy, happy college student from Chicago named Grace; Ted, an insurance salesman from Sheboygan; a goth girl named Shadeaux, and her goth boyfriend, Theo, who told us they were from "the darkness."

Rafael looked to be in his late thirties, with

a golden complexion, a black goatee, black eyebrows, and a gold hoop earring in one ear.

"You're all going to look frightened and nervous as you see Hackett Mansion for the first time," Rafael informed us.

"So we're almost there?" Deirdre asked excitedly.

"No," Rafael answered. "We're more than two hours away."

"But you want us to act excited *now*?" Ted asked.

"Yes. Yes, I do. Anticipate how afraid you're going to feel. Let fear seep into your bones and freeze your blood! Can you do that?" Rafael asked.

"Sure, I guess. I'll just imagine proposing to my girlfriend," Ted said. Bess, George, and I cracked up, but Deirdre just rolled her eyes.

"That's called method acting," Rafael told him. "You imagine something terrible and then you act as if it's really happening."

The two camera people turned around in their seats and trained their cameras on us. "Camera A" was L'Tinya Prescotte, who had on a faded T-shirt from another TV show and a pair of jeans. Zac "Camera B" Youngblood was tall, dark, and cool. He, too, wore jeans, a long-sleeved navy blue *Can*

You Hack It? T-shirt complete with an axe drip-ping blood, and a San Diego Padres baseball cap, worn backward. Both L'Tinya and Zac looked like they were in their mid-twenties.

"Go Padres," Bess murmured appreciatively. At the front of the bus, Zac grinned, and I won-dered if they had bugged our seats.

"And . . . action!" Rafael bellowed.

"Oh, good heavens!" Deirdre shrieked. "It's so frightening!"

"I think that's called method screaming," George said.

"That was excellent, Dorothy," Rafael told Deirdre. "But where were the rest of you? We need some energy, people! I want nerves! I want fear! I want second thoughts about what you are about to do—putting your lives on the line inside the blood-drenched walls of a haunted mansion built by a deranged madwoman! Be afraid, Hack-ees! Be very afraid! And . . . *action*!"

I slid a glance at George, who slid a glance back at me. "And the last drop of reality has left the building," George whispered.

We acted afraid, very afraid, for about an hour. Then Rafael noticed that Deirdre was getting hoarse, so he told us to relax.

I wished I could call Ned to tell him how

wacky our adventure into terror was so far, but Rafael had specifically ordered us not to bring any cell phones, MP3 players, radios, or electronic games. He wanted us to feel completely cut off from civilization as we walked the halls of Hackett Mansion.

"Here we are!" Rafael announced.

The bus downshifted on a little rise. Hackett Mansion lay dead ahead, and it was *creepy*. Looming against a gray, cloudy sky, dozens of jagged turrets and weather-beaten gables seemed to stare at us with hostile eyes. Smoke rose like breath from several chimneys, and the wide front door hung open like a mouth.

Rafael grinned from ear to ear.

"Pete, back up about twenty feet," he said. "Zac, get out and film our arrival. Deanndra, is it? Get your scream on again for me, baby."

"It's Deirdre," Deirdre corrected him, lifting her dark hair with her fingers as she smiled at him. "Like this?" She thrust out her lower lip and slapped her hands against her cheeks. "Oh, good heavens!"

"That's great. I love it," Rafael told her. "I see a girl who isn't afraid to be scared!"

"Oh, help me! Stop me from going in there!" Deirdre grabbed her throat.

"Fabulous! Magnificent!" Rafael shouted. "Camera A, get a close-up of this!"

"Blech," George said. "If I have to put up with this for a week, maybe I really will die in Hackett Mansion."

Zac and L'Tinya filmed us entering the mansion over and over, and each time I walked into the cobweb-strewn grand entrance, I felt a freezing *whoosh* that started at my heels and ended at the crown of my hair. George said she felt cold. Bess grew very quiet. Maybe we should have listened to Lucia's weird feelings about Hackett Mansion.

"I feel the vibes!" Deirdre shrieked, throwing herself into Ted's arms. Ted didn't mind. "I sense the evil of this place!"

"Good, good!" Rafael said. "This is great!"

I tried to shake off my odd reaction, reminding myself that I'd been investigating mysteries for years, and there had always been a logical explanation for everything I'd come up against, no matter how bizarre it seemed at first. But I couldn't shake the feeling that Lucia had been right: I shouldn't be here.

For the fifth time, I stepped into the unwelcoming entrance. The uneven floor creaked. High above us, shadows seemed to move and shift, and several passages disappeared off into the gloom. Okay, it looked spooky, but I had sleuthed in far less inviting places—junkyards, underground sewers, and an old, abandoned mine out West. I couldn't explain the uneasiness I felt, and as Lucia's worried face crossed my mind, I actually thought about getting back on the bus and leaving—the first Hackee who couldn't hack it.

Then I remembered that one woman had orchestrated the creation of this crazy place, and my love of a good mystery overcame my fear. I wanted to know what drove her to it. So I set down my suitcase (for the fifth time, under Rafael's direction) and gathered around our fear-loving leader with the others as he called us over.

By then, it had grown dark, and Zac and L'Tinya had placed lights all over the foyer. Some were clamped to stands and others hung from hooks fastened to a length of thick black cable strung along the wall. They didn't even have helpers to move the lights around, which I knew was pretty standard in Hollywood. I imagined this had to be a very low-budget production.

"Okay, Hackees," Rafael said in a spooky voice. "Here's your first horrifying adventure inside the haunted halls of Hackett House!"

Rafael snapped his fingers like a magician. Shadeaux and Theo, who had been coached on what to do, crouched on either side of a large piece of half-rotted, silvery fabric and lifted it up about an inch. We all knew something was underneath it, but we didn't know what.

"Hackett Silver," Rafael crooned, waving his hand in front of Zac's camera. "It was the cloth of kings and presidents. Sarah and Nathan Hackett were the only ones who knew how to make the fabulous cloth. In 1879, they built a textile mill right here on their property, where they spun the beautiful Hackett Silver. They became the multi-millionaires of Muskoka River."

Rafael's face clouded over. "In 1883, tragedy tore apart their web of good fortune when Nathan's lifeless body washed up on the riverbank. Some said that Sarah went insane from grief. Others claimed that guilt unhinged her mind—because she had murdered Nathan!"

"Oh," Deirdre gasped, pressing her hand against her chest. "How horrible!"

"Whatever the reason," Rafael continued, "that was when she started building this house, this crazed mansion with massive stairs that go up to the ceiling, two basements, six attics, the terrifying grand ballroom, and so many secret passageways and hidey-holes that no one has been able to explore them all."

"Oh, dear," Deirdre moaned. Zac swiveled his camera at her, then back to Rafael.

"Sarah stopped building in 1912. No one knows why. But six months later, she died. Coincidence?" Rafael asked.

"Probably not!" Deirdre half-screamed.

Rafael lowered his hand. That was Shadeaux and Theo's cue to slowly raise the piece of Hackett silver. Then Rafael grabbed it and tossed it over his shoulder, revealing ten lengths of rusty chain that led off in different directions. Attached to each piece was a fist-size plastic skull with our names written in "bloody" capital letters on the forehead. Zac zoomed in on them.

Bess's read B-E-T-H.

"Great," she groaned.

"It's time for you to explore Hackett Mansion," Rafael decreed. "Each of you, find your skull and follow the chain. It will lead you to your sleeping chamber . . . or should I say, your torture chamber?" He threw back his head. "Hahahahaha!"

Everyone, me included, bent down and picked up his or her chain. Mine trailed off to the left; George's went right, and Beth was supposed to go straight ahead.

I looked around to see where Deirdre was headed. Up the stairs. I thought of Evangeline Waters, and I couldn't help but smile.

"I know it's silly, but I'm a little scared," Bess murmured.

"It's total Hollywood," I reminded her, but I was feeling pretty uneasy myself.

"All right, Hackees, you're free to walk the halls of Hackett Mansion!" Rafael cried. "Rattle your chains and scream for your lives!"

"Eeeeeeeeeeeeeeeeeeeeeeeeeeeeeeeeeeeeeeek!" Deirdre shrieked.

"Yikes," I whispered.

Suddenly the walls shook with maniacal laughter. Thunder roared and lightning rumbled. The sound of rain spattered against the roof. The sound effects had kicked in.

A bright light followed me down a narrow corridor strewn with cobwebs. They looked real enough. So did the flies and bugs caught in them. The sound of dripping water echoed off the twisty-turn walls, and the floor was uneven and squeaked beneath my feet. Puffs of bone-chilling air hit my cheeks, and low, crazy laughter followed me everywhere.

It's just pretend, I thought. But the goose bumps on my arms and my fluttering heartbeat were certainly real.

★★★★

I didn't know if I was being filmed. If there were only two cameras and ten of us, we would probably have to do this only once. And once was more than enough for me. It was cold and dark; as I passed by a doorway, I could see the outline of someone standing on the threshold, staring silently at me.

As I moved on, another blast of icy air prickled my face and bony fingers tapped my shoulder. I whirled around, but there was no one there. I was shaking. I was seriously about to lose it, and I had only been in this place for two hours. I tried to distract myself.

I went into detective mode, trying to figure out how they created each special effect—a thin piece of filament? A clear piece of plastic? A dummy? Fake rats?—while at the same time, my teeth chattered and I dug my fists into my sweatshirt.

"*Nancy,*" a voice whispered in the darkness. "*Nancy Drew. I'm coming for you.*"

I licked my lips and found that my throat was so tight I couldn't make a sound in reply. I continued to follow the chain down the corridor. Another hallway intersected with it, and I hesitated. This was worse than the annual haunted house sponsored by the River Heights Chamber of Commerce; every Halloween season, the *Bugle* printed dozens of letters complaining that it was too scary.

I tried to remind myself that Rafael couldn't do anything that would actually hurt us. And then I heard Deirdre screaming, "No, no, no!" But this time, it sounded like she was in real trouble.

"Deirdre!" I shouted. "Are you all right?"

Gripping the length of chain in both my hands, I picked up speed. The light behind me kept pace. I was running now, through an open doorway, into a room that was dimly lit. There, I found George, Bess, and Deirdre staring down at an old-fashioned canopy bed. All their chains were bolted to the foot of the bed, and as I joined them, I saw old lady Sarah Hackett lying there, very wrinkled, with a huge splotch covering half her face, like a mask. Then she sat upright and shrieked at us.

We all screamed and jumped back. Deirdre grabbed on to Bess and buried her head against Bess's shoulder. George and I clutched each others' hands.

"And cut!" Rafael's boomed through the room. The shrieking stopped. The figure fell backward.

"Turn on the lights! Turn them on!" Deirdre cried.

"What's the matter, Deirdre? Can't you hack it?" Rafael's voice echoed all around us.

Then the bright light that had been following me blazed into the room. Still holding George's hand, I made myself look at the figure in the bed. It was a dummy, of course. I had seen pictures of Sarah Hackett in *Murder Mansion*, and Rafael and his crew had created a good likeness. Sarah Hackett had had a huge birthmark just like the one on the dummy, and many of her descendants had them as well.

Backlit by the bright light, Rafael walked into the room, chuckling at us. The light itself was attached to a helmet that Zac was wearing. He came in behind Rafael, slung his camera strap off his shoulder, and rested it against his hip.

"So, Deirdre, ready to go home?" Rafael persisted.

"I-I'm fine," Deirdre managed as she pulled herself out of Bess's arms and smoothed back her hair. "What are *you* looking at?" she snapped at us.

George, Bess, and I rolled our eyes at each other.

"Okay," Rafael said. "We've filmed Nancy on her walk through terror, so you can go have dinner, Nancy. Pete brought us all some fried chicken, mashed potatoes, and corn. It's waiting for you in the main entrance. We've also got some heaters going."

That sounded like heaven. It was so cold in the room that when I exhaled, I saw my breath.

"Wait a minute," Deirdre said. "All our chains led to this room. There is *one* bed in here. Are you saying we all have to sleep in this bed together?"

"Not exactly," Rafael said. "The bed will sleep two. And there are two sleeping bags." I craned my neck and looked around the opposite side of the bed. Sure enough, there were two sleeping bags . . . and another figure of Sarah Hackett identical to the one in the bed. She was propped up against the wall, staring right at me. I felt as if someone had poured ice water over the top of my head and it was running down my body.

"The figure in the bed will go, but the figure against the wall . . . stays all night."

"You're mean," Deirdre pouted.

"Screams mean ratings," Rafael replied, winking at her.

I turned to go. "Um, there's no light out there," I pointed out.

"It's okay. Just follow the chain," Rafael said casually. Then he winked at me. "And remember,

Pete is coming tomorrow to pick up anyone who can't hack it."

Not me, I thought, as I picked up my chain. Still, my heart thundered as I walked all the way back in the dark.

There were no puffs of air, no one touching me. I was so on edge waiting for someone to jump out at me that it was almost worse when no one did.

Who could sleep?

We drew straws to see who got the bed. Deirdre and I lost. We changed into pajamas and sweats and brushed our teeth. I tried not to think about the lifelike—or was that deathlike?—Sarah Hackett figure inches away from my sleeping bag as I snuggled inside the welcome warmth. But it was hard not to.

"This isn't fair," Deirdre said, rolling around inside her sleeping bag.

"We drew straws," I reminded her.

"No, I mean this whole thing. That Kate casting person made it sound like *fun*."

"You can go home," Bess said from the nice, soft, away-from-the-statue bed.

"Oh, you'd like that, wouldn't you? You would love to see me leave so *you* could star in Rafael's new horror movie! Well, trust me, Bess, you aren't going to!" She was quiet for a moment. And then another moment. Three. I almost started to relax.

"This isn't fair," she grumbled.

I didn't realize I had fallen asleep, but when I opened my eyes, I was staring straight into sunlight, so I must have dozed off at some point. Deirdre was still asleep, but I didn't see George or Bess in the bed.

Tonight that bed is mine, I thought happily.

That statue of Sarah Hackett had moved in the night—you mean someone moved her, Nancy. Now she was sitting at the foot of the bed. I ducked my eyes and avoided her as I walked through the room to the bathroom. I brushed my teeth and splashed very cold water on my face. No hot water. Joy.

We were supposed to meet in the dining room for breakfast. I thought I knew where the dining room was. But the door I thought I was supposed to use simply opened into the wall.

Next I tried a hall that dead-ended; then I took some stairs that went straight up to the ceiling. I went back down. I thought I was retracing my steps, but suddenly I found myself in a narrow, pitch-black passageway. Panicking a little, I wished I'd thought to bring a flashlight.

Then I heard a voice off to my right and saw a little circle of light through a knothole. I bent down and peered through it.

Dressed in a navy blue sweater, a jeans jacket, and jeans, a very tall, bony, baldheaded man about Rafael's age was walking across the room. He had a large birthmark that ran from just beneath his right temple to the corner of his mouth.

"They're going to find out, Noah," he said. "We've got to get them out of here."

Find out what? I thought. Who is he? Who is Noah? I stood as quietly as I could, listening. But he moved out of my range, and I couldn't hear anything else.

Then I saw a crack of light in front of me. It was a door. I turned the doorknob, went out, rounded a corner . . . and there was the dining room, which was decorated with ivy wallpaper and Greek statues.

"Hey, you made it!" George cried. There was a smattering of cheers and applause around the table. Everyone was eating breakfast sandwiches. Rafael was next to Deirdre; L'Tinya was seated beside Zac, who was filming. Zac glanced over at Bess and grinned.

I could practically feel the sparks flying between them and I grinned to myself. Bess is movie-star gorgeous with her classical oval face, blond hair, and blue eyes. Guys are always falling all over themselves around her. It could only be good for us if one of the insiders on the show took a liking to one of us Hackees.

However, in addition to the goo-goo eyes, I saw some awfully long faces.

Rafael walked over to Grace, placing a hand on her shoulder. She looked as if she hadn't slept at all.

"It seems that some of us couldn't hack our first night," Rafael said with an evil grin. "Hackett House has claimed its first three victims: Grace, and our twins, David and Chard. That leaves Nancy, Deirdre, George, Ted, Shadeaux, Theo, and Beth!"

"Bess," Bess whimpered.

Chard turned to the camera. "This place is totally bogus," he said. "It's too cold and it's dirty."

"It's too scary," Grace put in. "I can't hack it."

"Cut," Rafael said. He gave Grace a squeeze. "Good job. Loved it."

"Oh, good," Grace muttered.

"Okay, now that that's taken care of, finish your breakfasts and I'll unleash you on Murder Mansion."

"No." The man I had seen on the cell phone towered in the doorway. He was at least six foot four. "I don't want people going off by themselves."

Rafael raised a brow. "Oh, really? The production office said—"

"They lied," the man cut in.

"That's a strong accusation," Rafael ventured, and for the first time, he looked a little flustered. It didn't seem like an act. He turned to the rest of us with a fake smile plastered on his face. "Boys and girls, this is Jeremiah Hackett. He's the great-great-great grandnephew of Sarah and Nathan Hackett. He's here to oversee the production on behalf of the family."

"Hi, Jeremiah," Deirdre cooed, giving him a little wave. "This house is incredible."

He glared at her and didn't reply.

"You can't let them wander around on their own. It's too dangerous," he insisted.

"Why don't we discuss this privately?" Rafael said smoothly. "Everyone, take ten."

Zac, Rafael, and the two camerapeople left the room. Bess plopped down beside me. She gestured to George to come over.

"Okay, was that weird or what?" George said. "Do you think he's an actor, or is he really a

Hackett? I'm thinking he's real, because he is just as bizarre as this house. And did you see that strange marking on his face?"

"A lot of the Hacketts had large birthmarks," I said. "They inherited them from Sarah Hackett."

"All right, everyone, change of plans," Rafael announced, clapping his hands together as he came back into the room with Jeremiah. "We're going to explore the attic together. Perhaps we will find some skeletons there. Wahaha."

I could see that he was trying to get back into his "scary guy" persona, but it wasn't working. He was genuinely upset.

"Come on, come on, slowpokes!" Rafael urged us, breaking up our private discussion. "What's the matter? Didn't you get enough sleep last night?"

Single file, we wound around and around a circular staircase of super-creaky stairs. Deirdre was just behind Rafael, then George, then Bess, then me, and Ted and the goths were behind me. The twins and Grace all opted out, preferring to take it easy near the heaters while they waited for Pete to show up and drive them back to River Heights.

I felt another puff of cold air against my cheek, just like last night; and I glanced to the left, to see an oil portrait of Sarah Hackett wearing a silvery veil that concealed most but not all of her birthmark, staring back at me from the wall. Her eyes seemed to lock gazes with me, not in a scary way, but as if she really had something to tell me. Then I saw a small hole drilled into the base of the picture. I covered it, and felt a puff of air against my fingertip. Some kind of motion-sensitive air blower had been inserted into the painting.

Then Deirdre screamed really, really loudly.

"My cheek!" she cried. "Something bit me!"

My natural protective instincts kicked in and I pushed my way up the staircase to Deirdre. She had sunk down onto a stair with both her hands pressed against her cheek. "Let me see," I said.

She pulled her hand away uncertainly. "Am I bleeding?" she cried. "It really hurts!"

"Cut. Cameras off," Rafael ordered. "I'm sure it's just a scratch," he added nervously, although he hadn't even seen it.

It *was* just a scratch, but I would have been freaking out too, if it had happened to me. I trailed my flashlight to the same side of the wall as the portrait. Sure enough, there was a little hole in the wood paneling. I put my forefinger over it, and felt a sharp sting.

"Ow!" I cried, jerking my finger away. In the beam of my flashlight, I saw a splinter imbedded beneath the skin.

"This one shoots out splinters," I told Rafael.

"No way," he replied, turning red.

"What are you talking about?" Deirdre asked.

"See?" I took my pencil flashlight out of my jeans pocket and aimed it so that she could see the little hole. "Watch." I waved my hand in front of the hole, quickly jerking it back so I wouldn't catch any splinters.

"Very clever," Rafael said. "You figured out one of our special effects. I'm impressed."

"Nancy's a detective," George informed Rafael. "Nancy Drew. She's famous in River Heights. She'll figure out how you perform all your special effects in no time."

"Oh, really?" He raised a brow and grinned at me mischievously. "We can incorporate that into our show—have a little 'Nancy Drew moment' where you explain how we created our thrills and chills."

"Um, hello? Injured?" Deirdre snapped, pointing to her cheek.

"It's a wood splinter, all right," Rafael said. "If you want, we can fill out an accident form and take you to see a doctor." He looked very sad.

"I'm afraid if we do that, it will mean you're off the show."

"*Oh.*" She straightened her shoulders. "Well, for the good of the show . . . after all, it *is* just a scratch."

The trip to the attic was loaded with thrills and chills, Hollywood style—glowing skeletons dropping from the ceiling and extremely eerie sound effects like echoing laughter and more thunder and lightning. A trapdoor in the floor opened and Zac popped out, wearing a hockey mask and holding a chain saw.

Deirdre screamed her head off and George and Bess jumped a few times. The goths looked a little bored and started muttering to each other about going home.

After disappearing for most of the day, Jeremiah Hackett started following us everywhere we went. It was obvious he didn't want us in the house. It was also evident—at least to me—that he was very tightly wound. He paced and shifted like someone who has had way too much caffeine, and every now and then he would take out his cell phone and flip it open to check what time it was. Then he would stuff it in his pocket and glare.

At me.

★★★★

Finally it was time to go to bed, our second night in the house.

"I've taken pity on you four," Rafael told George, Bess, Deirdre, and me. "I've decided it was unfair to make two of you sleep on the floor when Miss Sarah built so many rooms." He smiled. "So each of you will have her own room tonight!"

"Yay?" George said uncertainly.

"Oh, Rafael, I really don't mind if the girls sleep on my floor," Deirdre told him.

Rafael held up his hands and grimaced in a mock apology. "Sorry, but the plans have been set in motion. Remember, stay snug in your beds. We'll leave the hallways to the ghosts tonight."

Rafael assigned us all rooms that were far apart from one another. In my room, red velvet wallpaper was half ripped away from the walls, and furniture was shrouded in white sheets coated with dust. At least I had fresh sheets on the narrow, dark red divan Rafael had assigned to be my bed.

I brushed my teeth and climbed into my sweats. Then I crawled onto the divan. I put on my old black mittens and by the light of my flashlight, I took out my black leather clue notebook and tried to sketch a layout of the house. I propped *Murder Mansion* on my knees, comparing my sketch to a couple of pages in the book that were supposed to be the original blueprints of the house. I was edgy, waiting for Rafael to scare me. I tried to relax by taking deep breaths, and at some point I realized I was actually beginning to doze.

"Nancy Drew," a voice whispered.

I opened one eye. "Microphone. Sound system," I said, and closed my eye.

"Nancy Drew."

"I'm sleeping," I said.

"Nancy?" The voice was louder. It was Deirdre. "Nancy, can you come to my room? I think something's in here!"

"It's just Hollywood," I mumbled, but she whimpered, so I sat up, slipped on my flats, grabbed my pencil flashlight and the book, open to the blueprints of the floor plans, and left my room. I was aware I was violating the new rule to travel in groups, but I decided to take my chances. As irritating as Deirdre might be sometimes, I would never turn her down if she seriously asked for my help.

The Sarah Hackett doll was sitting in the hall, facing my door.

"Ha ha," I said, for the camera's benefit . . . wherever it might be.

I started down the hall, shivering, wishing I had put on a jacket. I aimed my flashlight left and right, searching for a sliver of light beneath a door.

I heard my name again, behind the door to my right, but it wasn't Deirdre who spoke it. Creeping closer, I listened.

"Nancy Drew. She shouldn't be here." It was Jeremiah Hackett.

"Why not?" Rafael asked. "We love her. We love that she's an amateur detective. We're working out how to use that in the show."

"I don't like her."

Footsteps stomped toward the door and the doorknob turned. Someone—probably Jeremiah—was coming into the hall.

I turned off my flashlight and whirled around to go back, but the door creaked open, so I trotted along the wall, feeling for another doorknob. As soon as I found one, I turned it, and opened the door. I jumped across the threshold and pulled the door nearly closed.

Heavy footfalls made the floor vibrate. I waited a few more minutes, then moved to crack open the door so I could see if the coast was clear.

But the door didn't open. Somehow I must have pushed it closed without realizing it. I tried the knob, but it had somehow locked as well. So I flicked my flashlight back on to examine the mechanism.

But my flashlight didn't turn on. Anxiety prickled the back of my neck. I was trapped in the dark, in what appeared to be another secret passageway, with no light.

And then I heard a floorboard creak about ten feet behind me. Someone was in the passageway.

"Is someone in here?" It was Jeremiah.

Great, I thought nervously. I really didn't want to come face to face with him in the dark. So I abandoned the door and tiptoed forward, turning a corner just as a bloom of light bounced off the wall. *His* flashlight was working just fine.

Years of detective work had taught me a lot about how to walk soundlessly, but I knew this was an old house and one of the floorboards could creak at any moment. At one point my forehead brushed an overhang; after that, I kept my hand raised over my head. Lucky thing: the ceiling abruptly dropped down to maybe five feet—I'm five seven—and I had to bend over as I walked.

I nearly tumbled down a flight of stairs. When I reached the bottom, my flashlight turned back on, and I found myself standing in a doorway.

I was looking into a filthy room made entirely out of rock. Dust at least two inches thick coated the rock floor. There were some old, disintegrated wooden crates pushed against a wall. They were marked HACKETT SILVER, and something that looked like swatches of fabric had fallen out of them.

Cautiously, I glided over and examined one of the crates with my flashlight. I used the edge of the book to move some of the fabric, in case there were rats or spiders underneath. Then I lifted up a piece. It tore loose from the rest of the material. I gave it a good shaking—dust clouds billowed like ghosts—and wiped it with my fingertips. The sheen of Hackett Silver was dimly visible.

I had jumped at the chance to come to mysterious Hackett Mansion to learn why Sarah Hackett had built it for so long. But now I was equally interested in finding out what Jeremiah Hackett—and "Noah"—were hiding. But right now, I had to get back to Deirdre. So I gathered up the shreds of Hackett Silver and dropped little bits on the floor as I retraced my steps, marking my trail. That way, I could come back at a better time and get back to sleuthing.

Soon I had returned to my starting place. Jeremiah Hackett was nowhere to be seen, so I crept back to the door I had originally passed through. This time it unlocked with ease. I slowly opened it—and a flashlight shone directly in my face.

"Where have you *been*?" Deirdre whined. "I have been calling and calling for you!"

The next morning, Rafael announced that the seven of us Hackees were all still in the game. Rafael screened two of his horror movies for us in the grand ballroom. They were *Horror House* and *Horror House II*, and I have to say that I didn't much care for them. They were mostly excuses for girls to run around screaming until they met a very gory death.

"So you're doing all this to be in one of *those*?" George muttered at Bess.

"Some of the finest actresses in the industry got their start in horror movies," Bess replied, chewing her lower lip. "Eww," she added, as another blond girl died in a truly inventive way.

I glanced over at Jeremiah, who was sprawling in a big, half-rotten, red velvet chair. Every time someone got killed, he chuckled. It was unnerving how much he was enjoying all the splattery gore.

George and I traded glances.

The next day—the third—wasn't as freaky as the first two, at least by *Can You Hack It?* standards. Oh, Rafael still elicited an eardrum-piercing shriek out of Deirdre by jumping out of a closet. Bess almost fainted when he used the old "Pepper's Ghost" parlor trick using statues and mirrors to make ghosts appear to glide through the air. Afterward, while Bess calmed down, he filmed me explaining how it worked.

It was a little bit of a surprise on the morning of the fourth day when Shadeaux and Theo announced that they couldn't hack it any more.

"Actually, we had to decide between coming to this and attending a gothic literature festival," Shadeaux said. "We can still make the festival. Books have a little more depth than reality shows."

"So there you have it!" Rafael said into the camera. "Our thrills and chills are shallow!" But his attempt at a joke fell pretty flat.

George, Deirdre, Bess, and I huddled out of range to the right, where a fire was blazing in the fireplace. It was nice and warm. That left just Ted, who started trying to sell life insurance to Zac, L'Tinya, and Rafael. Rafael thought that was so funny that he decided to film it. He sat Ted down in an old moth-eaten chair and positioned some lights on him.

"And . . . action," he said, moving off to the left. Zac took a step forward, training his camera on Ted.

"What if you *do* die here in Hackett Mansion?" Ted asked. "You don't want to leave your loved ones in the lurch!"

Jeremiah walked into the room and stood behind Zac, observing. He scowled. Then he pushed Zac out of the way and stomped toward the chair.

"That's not funny!" he shouted. "That's sick! This whole thing is sick!" Then he bent down and grabbed a cardboard box Zac had gotten some fresh batteries out of and hurled it at the wall above Ted's head. Ted ducked.

"People die, you know!" Jeremiah yelled. He looked around and grabbed a wooden chair. "They die in terrible ways! Or haven't you been watching?"

Then he slammed the chair against the wall. "They die, and it's terrible, and you shouldn't make fun!"

"Hey, Jeremiah, guy, let's take it easy," Rafael said, as he held out his hands. "It's just a good time, right? A TV show."

"You're making fun of dying!" Jeremiah shouted, grabbing his head, then flinging his hands down at his sides. "Making jokes about life insurance!"

"Well, I really do sell life insurance," Ted began nervously. "Um . . ."

"Let's try this again some other time," Rafael said. "Jeremiah, let's go have a chat. See if we can't find a happy space for both of us."

"Happy space?" Deirdre said, watching them go. "How about an insane asylum?"

"Look, you guys," I told the girls. "This is getting weird. I think we should leave."

"No way!" Deirdre said.

Bess shook her head.

"Please, Nancy, he's not so bad."

"Yeah," Deirdre said. "Don't mess this up for me."

"I'm with Nancy," George announced. "I'm cold and I need a hot shower. And Jeremiah is scary."

"How can you not care about being on TV?" Bess asked.

"Like this." George stared at her. "See? This is me not caring."

"Maybe you should say you can't hack it so you can leave," I suggested to George. "Then go to Chief McGinnis and ask him to get the local law to pay us a visit." The chief of the River Heights Police Department and I had solved many cases, not exactly together—and I usually let the chief take all the credit. That way he didn't squawk too loudly when I poked around on my own.

"You cannot bring any police into this!" Deirdre protested. "Nancy, what if some ignorant trooper guy comes out here and orders Rafael to shut down?"

"Maybe you should say that *you* can't hack it too," George said to me. "You speak the chief's lingo better than me."

"No," Bess said. "Nancy knows how they make all their special effects. If you're not here to explain them to me, I'll go insane."

"I think Bess is right," Deirdre told me. "You should go too."

"How about a compromise?" I suggested. "George goes tomorrow morning and checks in with *Ned*. They do some checking into Jeremiah Hackett. If they come up with anything, they check with Chief McGinnis, and he can call Rafael."

"Wouldn't it be easier just to call Ned from

here?" George ventured. "Bess, you could flutter your lashes at Zac and ask to borrow his phone."

"No!" Deirdre and Bess chorused.

"Phone use is expressly forbidden," Deirdre said.

"Then *I'll* ask, after I tell him I can't hack it," George said.

"No, no, no!" Bess pleaded. "Rafael might kick *all* of us off the show."

"Why all of us? Just because we're friends?" I asked.

"I wouldn't go *that* far," Deirdre said snootily. "But he does know we're together. If he thinks we plotted to use a phone, which is against the rules . . ." She lowered her voice. "For all we know, he may be apingtay usay ightray ownay."

"Pig Latin?" George snorted. "Come *on*! All right, I'll tell him I can't hack it, and talk to Ned."

So George left the next morning. Then it was just Deirdre, Bess, Ted, and me. And Jeremiah and the crew, of course. Everyone tiptoed around Jeremiah, but when he wasn't around, Rafael, Zac, and L'Tinya were all giddy and secretive, and I just knew they had something scary planned for us.

Yay, I thought nervously.

★★★★

"Nancy?"

That night, I was drifting off to sleep on my narrow divan when I heard Deirdre calling my name again. Someday I had to remember to ask her why she came to me for help when she disliked me so much. But I'd save that for another time.

I knew the route to the hall by then, so I didn't take *Murder Mansion* or my sketch with me. I did, however, bring a backup flashlight, and I wore a jacket.

And then, just like the second night, I heard Jeremiah Hackett. Only this time he was behind a different closed door.

"Don't you tell them, Sarah Hackett. Don't you say a word," he said. "What? No, I will not confess!"

"Deirdre?" I whispered.

She flicked on her flashlight. "Nancy, do you hear him? He's talking to Sarah Hackett! Or at least he thinks he is. Do you think he's faking it or do you think we are out here with a lunatic?"

"I'm not sure," I said honestly.

The next morning, I went to Rafael and asked to speak to him privately. We met in a dimly lit room filled with lighting equipment, coils of cable, and the two Sarah Hackett figures, both seated on a settee. He sat beside one of them and held her hand. I sat across from him in a chair.

"You're not leaving today, are you?" he asked anxiously. "We purposely didn't scare you guys last night so you'd stick around. We won't do anything to you tonight, either. We really like you four. Tomorrow night will be the grand finale. Then I want to do a final segment where you and I talk about our special effects."

"We're really worried about Jeremiah," I told him. "We heard him talking to himself in his room. Did you get him to do that?"

"No," Rafael said, "and he won't even let me use any of it. What a waste."

I stared at him. "Maybe it's a waste to you, but we're scared."

He smiled at me. "You can't hack it." Then he stopped smiling. "But I need you to hack it. You're my Nancy-star, Nancy Drew! I need you."

I didn't want to push too hard. I knew Bess—and Deirdre—really wanted a shot at being in the movie.

"Look, tomorrow night is the last night of filming," he said. "I have a special guest flying in. She can't get here any sooner. She's fully booked. I will do everything I can to make sure Jeremiah doesn't flip out again. I promise, promise, promise you." He laced his hands together and held them out to me. "I am begging you. I will guarantee you a role in my next horror movie."

"I'm not really a horror movie kind of girl," I told him. "But Bess and Deirdre are."

He exhaled. "I don't know why they want to be in a horror movie so badly. I sure don't want to make another one. I came to Hollywood with a different plan, that's for sure. I was going to make a difference." He smiled wryly. "Pesky rent. Pesky car payments."

He cocked his head. "Look, I could save some money if we didn't film today. You guys could relax and enjoy the thoroughly creepy and disgusting house you have been forced to live in for five days," he said merrily.

And I could get back downstairs to investigate those crates, I realized. Maybe I'll also figure out what Jeremiah's game is—something that doesn't require a full deck, that's for sure.

"Seriously, we will watch Jeremiah. One weird move, and we'll get you out of here," Rafael said.

"Okay. Just one weird move." I held up a finger.

"Good. Let's shake on that, Nancy Drew."

I took his hand. Then he stood up, chuckling, and I saw that I was holding the hand of the Hackett doll beside him.

"Gotcha," he said, grinning at me.

I grinned back to show there were no hard feelings. Then I found the girls and told them the plan.

"Cool," Deirdre said. "Movie parts if we stay." She smiled at the others. "We can do this, ladies."

"And meanwhile, I've been trying to solve the mystery of why Sarah Hackett kept building on to the house," I said. I told them about the crates I had seen down in the basement.

"Let's go see them," George said. "We have nothing else to do all day."

We waited to see if Jeremiah was around, but Rafael told us he'd just left with Pete to go on some errands and wasn't going to come back tonight. We were incredibly relieved. So were Rafael, Zac, and L'Tinya, who became engrossed in something that looked technical and potentially scary. Ted wanted to watch more horror movies. That left us on our own.

I led the way through the twists and turns of the inner passageway, showing them my bits of Hackett Silver. Deirdre started to gather them up.

"Leave them, please," I told her. "That way, I can come back again."

"Why would you want to?" Deirdre grumbled, shuddering as we ducked beneath the low ceiling.

"Because I love a good mystery," I told her.

But when we got to the room where I had seen the crates, there was a new mystery: What had happened to them?

The room was completely bare.

We went back upstairs. It was getting dark.

"No screams tonight," Rafael said. "I promise."

"Thanks," I said. "And by the way, I would like to use your phone to make a call." I wanted to double-check with Ned to see if he'd come up with anything about Jeremiah.

He laughed. "Nancy, are you kidding? We don't have cell phone reception way out here. We haven't used our phones once since we set up shop."

"Jeremiah Hackett has," I countered. "I've seen him." Then a chill ran down my spine. Because I *hadn't* actually seen him use his phone. Maybe this Noah was in the house!

"Either he's got a better cell phone service provider," I said, "he's a little crazier than we realized, or someone else is in the house."

"Oh, my God. I'm going to talk to Ted and Zac," Rafael said. "I'll get back to you."

A few hours later, shadows spread across the walls and floors of Hackett Mansion, bleeding the color out of our faces as Rafael sat across from us at the dining room table.

"We've searched the entire house," Rafael said, "and I promise you, there is no one here. Unless he or she is invisible," he added. As Deirdre whimpered, he reached across the table and patted her arm. "Sorry, I just can't stop myself."

We four went to sleep in the room with the canopy bed, adding my divan and a couch for George. George's couch was about a foot away from mine. Deirdre and Bess were sharing the canopy bed. I had just settled in and was beginning to drop off when George reached over and squeezed my hand. I smiled and squeezed back.

Then George said from the doorway, "Does anyone have any floss?"

I bolted up and grabbed my flashlight, shining it at George's couch. Her empty couch. I stared down at my hand.

"Who was just holding my hand?" I blurted.

But no one knew.

Nor did anyone sleep for the rest of the night.

★★★★

"Last day, everybody," Rafael said into the camera the next morning at breakfast. As if any of us had to be reminded. "We're going to have a séance tonight. Pete will be standing by in case it's just so terrifying you have to leave immediately."

Jeremiah came back—not with Pete, but in a taxi. I wondered why he hadn't come with Pete.

"Pete had to go to the airport to pick up our special guest," Rafael explained.

Zac, L'Tinya, and Rafael worked for the rest of the day getting the house ready for the séance, but at all times, one of them "happened" to be near Jeremiah. The séance was going to be held in the grand ballroom. They set a large table covered with a black velvet cloth in the center of the room, then spent a long time adjusting red and blue gels over lights to set an eerie mood. Rafael spent an equally long time working on some "surprises."

Jeremiah got very agitated once he heard there was going to be a séance. He tried to forbid Rafael to do it, but this time, Rafael stood his ground.

"It was in our original contract with your family's attorney," Rafael said.

"It's not right," Jeremiah insisted. "You can't do it!"

I went to Rafael again. "Is there any way I can

talk you into just stopping now?" I asked him.

"What can he do?" Rafael asked. "We're all here watching him." He lowered his voice. "Zac went through his luggage. He's got a secret stash of chocolate chip cookies, but that's it. There's no *body* named Noah in his suitcase."

"You have a very twisted sense of humor," I told him.

"That's why I got this gig," he replied.

"We are not skipping the séance," Deirdre said, coming up behind us. "And I hope that you have disqualified Nancy from becoming Scream Queen."

"I don't want to be Scream Queen," I told Rafael.

Rafael's shoulders slumped. "If this show doesn't get some decent ratings, I won't need a Scream Queen."

"The séance is happening, and that's final, Nancy Drew," Deirdre insisted. She gazed at Rafael. "And I am screaming like you've never heard before."

"That makes me very happy," he told her, sounding kind of weary.

"Madame Zelonka," the psychic who was supposed to lead the séance, didn't show at eight, when she was due. Her real name was Leah

Goldberg, and she didn't arrive until nearly eleven.

"Your driver never showed up, Rafey," she chastised Rafael as Zac wheeled in a suitcase for her. "I had to rent a car." She was dressed in a long, black gown with lots of gold chains, and black hair trailing down past her hips.

"I am so sorry, Mrs. Goldberg." Rafael looked worried. "What could have happened?" He went off to talk to Zac and L'Tinya.

I had a bad thought. We really had no way of knowing if George and Pete got back to River Heights safely. . . .

"Listen, girls, we're gonna really pump up the volume for Rafael tonight, okay? Such a nice boy; I know his mother." She shook her head. "This isn't how he started out, you know? He wanted to do good things with film, help people. Me, I don't care so much."

This is his very special guest? I thought. I guess that's show biz.

She pulled a crystal ball out of her suitcase. Jeremiah slunk past her, scowling at her.

She made a face at his departing back. "That one throws off bad vibes."

Madame Zelonka, Zac, L'Tinya, and Rafael continued getting ready for the séance. I offered

111

to help, but Rafael said he wanted there to be *some* chills and thrills left.

Then, as we sat around, I saw Jeremiah pull his phone out of the pocket of a hooded sweatshirt and depress the keys. He was *texting*. Maybe he did have superior cell phone service . . . or maybe he was communicating with the great beyond. With Jeremiah, there was no way to tell.

So far, anyway, I reminded myself. I had not given up on solving the mystery of Jeremiah Hackett.

At around 11:30, everyone convened in the ballroom, except Jeremiah. It was freezing, and Rafael had refused to bring any heaters in. He insisted that it would add to the "reality" to see our breath in the air. So we all came in bundled in jackets. I wore my mittens, too.

"Where is he?" Rafael gritted, then sighed with relief as Jeremiah strode in, wearing a plain black hooded sweatshirt and black gloves.

I looked at Rafael as if to say, *You lost track of him?!*

He grimaced an apology.

Lightning crackled outside, and inside, candles ringed a perimeter around the table.

"Sit down," Madame Zelonka said, in a very Gypsy-like voice. "Join hands."

Probably to everyone's surprise—including Jeremiah's—I sat down next to him and placed "my" left-mittened hand in his right. Only it wasn't my hand. It was the hand from Sarah Hackett's dummy—the one Rafael had used to tease me. I had loaded it into the arm of my jacket, leaving my own hand free.

"We will now close our eyes to summon the spirits," she continued.

That was *my* cue to slip my hand very, very carefully into the pocket of Jeremiah's jacket, in hopes of finding his cell phone.

He shifted in his chair. I froze. But he kept his eyes closed.

There! My fingertips brushed hard metal. I slipped the phone into my jeans pocket.

"Open your eyes," Madame Zelonka said.

"Whoa," Ted murmured.

The ghostly form of Sarah Hackett hovered above the table. I followed the angle and figured that Rafael had used another reflecting mirrors trick. He caught my eye and raised a brow.

I smiled back.

Wind blew through the room, ruffling my hair, followed by crashing lightning, rumbling thunder, and pouring rain. Whispers bounced off the walls, and I heard the sound of footfalls echoing off the floor. Even I, who knew the effects were fake, felt as if fingers made of ice cubes were climbing up my spine.

"I am Sarah Hackett," whispered a voice. "For nearly a hundred years I have walked these halls . . . and now I will reveal the secrets of Hackett Mansion to you."

"Sarah, don't," Jeremiah said aloud. Zac swiveled his camera onto him. "Sarah, be quiet."

More wind blew, and I caught the faint odor of . . . smoke?

Suddenly Madame Zelonka's head fell back and her eyes turned milky white!

"I am Sarah Hackett, and this house is filled with vile pestilence. The earth is poisoned. Fish die, birds die . . . we all die . . . " Her voice sounded old and frail, not like Mrs. Goldberg's voice at all.

"Shut up, Sarah!" Jeremiah shouted, jumping off his chair. It clattered on the floor as he leaped at Madame Zelonka.

"Hey!" Ted and Rafael said, grabbing his arms.

"Fire," said the eerie voice issuing out of Mrs. Goldberg's mouth. *"Run."*

As the men wrestled Jeremiah to the ground, smoke suddenly poured into the room. Coughing, I gazed up . . . to find flames dancing along the ceiling!

"Fire!" I shouted, pointing.

In her chair, Mrs. Goldberg coughed and blinked her eyes. She took one look at the ceiling and scrambled out of her chair.

"Rafey!" she cried. "This is too much!"

"These are not special effects! This is really happening! People, we need to clear the set!" Rafael shouted, taking her hand. "Follow me!"

A flaming section of the ceiling detached and barely missed Deirdre's head. Another plummeted to the floor, and another.

"Help!" Deirdre screamed, racing from the room.

"Stay with the group!" Rafael yelled at her.

"Deirdre, stop!" I shouted, but as I moved out of the ballroom, I saw that the entire house was catching fire. I remembered Jeremiah's phone in my jeans and dialed 911. "Hello! Fire, Hackett Mansion!" I shouted. I couldn't tell if the call went through. As I ran, I called my dad, then Ned's number, but I couldn't be sure if those had gone through either. I stood still for a second, weighing what to do, when Bess collided with me.

"Nancy!" Bess bellowed. The place is going up! Let's get out of here!"

"Help!" I heard Deirdre shrieking. "Help me!"

"Come with me," I told Bess, grabbing her hand. "Deirdre! Keep shouting!"

"Nancy!"

"Let's go to the left," I told Bess. We ran down the hall where Deirdre's room was located. Fire raced behind and ahead of us, threatening to squeeze us in the middle. As smoke swirled and thickened, I spotted Deirdre waving her arms, coughing, and choking.

"Deirdre, here we are!" I told her.

By the time she ran to us, our way back was blocked. Then I recognized the door I had hidden behind, the one that led into the secret passage. I felt it, making sure the knob wasn't hot; then I yanked it open and pushed Deirdre and Bess inside.

I shut the door. I had my pencil flashlight and I turned it on. I saw the pieces of Hackett Silver I had dropped on the floor. I shined my flashlight on each piece as we raced along. We reached the overhang, and the stairs, and I got them into the basement. I tried the phone, but there was no reception in the room made of rock.

In the room that had previously held the crates, something square and black lay on the floor. A book. I picked it up, and dropped it into my jacket pocket. Then Bess pushed me out of the way as part of the ceiling collapsed, and huge chunks of ceiling rumbled down in a cascade.

"We can't stay here," I shouted, darting back out of the room. But clouds of thick smoke were pouring down the stairway as if they were chasing after us. Deirdre was screaming so loudly I couldn't think straight—until the smoke caught us. Then she doubled over, coughing hard.

Fanning the smoke out of my face, I ran my flashlight to the left and the right, but all I saw were vortexes of smoke. My eyes were burning, I was coughing, and I didn't know what to do.

And then I felt someone tugging on my jacket.

"This way," a voice whispered softly in my ear.

"Come on," I told Bess and Deirdre. I dragged them to the left. There was a solid wall there and I began to slow, but the *someone* tugged on my jacket again.

"It's a dead end," Deirdre said, but when I got to the wall, a panel slid open. How had it done that on its own?

But there was no time to think. I crawled through the now-open panel into another crazy maze of passages, deep inside Hackett Mansion.

Through twists and turns, I forced Bess and Deirdre to keep up. We wound up in a narrow crawlspace brimming with smoke, and I started to panic. What if I had been tricked into going the wrong way? The smoke was taking its toll on us; I punched in 911 over and over again, yelling *"Hackett Mansion! Fire!"* in case anyone could hear me.

Eventually, we burst out of the little passageway into smoke-clogged darkness. I had no idea where we were, but at least we weren't stuffed into a tiny passageway any longer.

"Come on, let's go," I shouted at the two girls.

"I can't . . . oh . . ." Deirdre went limp and slumped to the floor.

"Help me!" I ordered Bess. Fumbling and coughing, she and I slung our arms underneath Deirdre's arms. I could only half-stand. My eyes were burning. I couldn't get enough air into my lungs.

Suddenly, I felt someone holding on to my jacket, guiding my steps. I stumbled forward and nearly fell, but whoever was helping me grabbed my forearm and kept me upright.

Just when I thought I couldn't go any farther, I felt cool air and dragged Deirdre toward it.

"Come, Nancy Drew," a voice said.

I kept going. Then I stepped through a doorway and into the night. We were out.

I turned around, to see the entire crazy Hackett mansion on fire as Deirdre fell onto her knees, coughing.

"Thank you!" I shouted, collapsing beside her. I threw back my head and gulped in air. Then I realized that Rafael and the others might be trapped inside.

Coughing and hacking, I slowly got to my feet.

The phone rang!

It was Ned.

"Ned, the mansion is on fire," I rasped. The phone was beeping, signaling a low battery. "We're out. I don't know about the others."

"I'll call the fire department," he said. "We're coming, Nancy."

Then the phone went dead.

"Stay here," I told Deirdre and Bess. "I have to see if I can help."

"No!" they both yelled, but I staggered forward. I saw Rafael, Zac, and L'Tinya coming around the side of the burning mansion, waving their arms.

Then I guess I collapsed.

When I came to, I was lying on a stretcher, staring up at the blazing inferno that had once been

Hackett Mansion, a hundred yards away. Six fire engines and at least as many ambulances were on the scene. Firefighters in yellow uniforms wielded hoses against the flames, but I guessed it was hopeless.

My dad, Ned, George, and Chief McGinnis were standing around me and I smiled at them. George was safe.

"Oh, Nancy," my dad said, squeezing me tight. "Thank God you're all right."

"Everyone got out," Ned told me, wrapping me up in his arms. "Bess and Deirdre are being treated for smoke inhalation, but they're going to be okay."

"Jeremiah Hackett is in custody," my dad added. "He confessed to setting the fire by using the gasoline in the tank of Mrs. Goldberg's rental car."

"He had an accomplice, or a partner or something," I said. "Noah."

"Already looked into," Chief McGinnis informed me. "Noah Hackett was his younger brother. He died last year, mysteriously."

"Pete," I said. "The driver—"

"He had engine trouble on the way to the airport. He couldn't tell anyone at the mansion because of the phone problem, and Mrs. Goldberg didn't hear the airport paging her," George said.

I closed my eyes in sheer relief. It could have ended so badly. Hackett Mansion might be gone, but everyone connected to *Can You Hack It?* was safe.

"I know Jeremiah set the fire because he didn't want anyone to know the secret of Hackett Mansion," I said. "But what *is* the secret? Did he tell you?" In spite of everything, my "mystery-dar" was up and running.

"It's in here," my dad said. He held out the book I had found in the basement. The pages were mildewed and brittle, and my eyes were sore and burning, but I read where he pointed.

> *The ghosts are coming for me. Hackett Silver itself has poisoned the earth, the river, and our very souls. My vegetable garden, my chickens . . . the fish Nathan caught. We suspected it for years, but we wanted the fortune it gave us. People downriver began to sicken and die, but we said nothing.*
>
> *Then the poison attacked us—our limbs, and our very minds. Nathan was not himself when he leaped to his death in the river. And now his ghost haunts me—and all the ghosts of those downriver. And the birds, and the animals of the forest. Blaming me for never speaking up.*

I must hide from them. Trick them, so when they search for me in the night, they will not find me. I saw a ghost just tonight, gliding beneath the moon. He called to me: "Sarah Hackett. We will find you. No matter where you hide, we will come for you."

So *that* was why she had kept building onto the house! She was trying to find a place to hide.

"The land is polluted?" I asked. "If the Hackett descendants didn't want anyone to know, why did they give permission for Rafael to shoot here?"

"Apparently they didn't know either," Chief McGinnis replied.

"George and I went on the Internet yesterday," Ned said. "We found a few things. Jeremiah and Noah commissioned a land survey at Hackett Mansion. Maybe they were hoping to sell the property. We don't know. The surveyor who conducted the survey appears to have died, also under mysterious circumstances, like Noah."

"So the surveyor discovered that the land is polluted?" I asked.

"That will have to be investigated," Chief McGinnis replied.

Just then Mrs. Goldberg was wheeled over to

me on a gurney by two paramedics. She pulled the oxygen mask off her face and reached out for my hand.

"I made real contact," she said hoarsely, giving me a squeeze. "First time in my entire career. She wants you to know she's at peace now. She doesn't have to hide any more."

"Who?" my dad asked.

Mrs. Goldberg and I shared a look.

Almost a year to the day after the fire, Bess, George, Ned, Hannah, Evangeline, and yes, even Deirdre, joined us at our house for berry pie (made with pesticide-free berries from our garden!) to watch Rafael's show. He had turned *Can You Hack It?* into a documentary exposing the dark secret of Hackett Mansion. Because of the documentary, he'd gotten a deal with PBS to make an entire series of documentaries about "Foul Places." He was finally getting to do what he had always wanted to do—make a difference.

"Come with me now," Rafael beckoned from the screen. He stood in front of the ashes of Hackett Mansion, which were surrounded by a chain link fence with a big sign on it. It read BIOHAZARD. DO NOT ENTER.

"Come see the terrible secret Jeremiah Hackett

tried to hide—that the chemicals that Hackett Silver created drove Nathan Hackett into the river, and his widow to build a mansion for thirty years, in hopes of eluding those harmed by their turn-of-the-century industrial waste.

"Jeremiah Hackett wanted to keep the family skeleton in the closet, and he murdered anyone who could reveal the truth."

"He hasn't lost his terrible sense of melodrama," George said, grinning crookedly.

"Someday I'll be in a movie," Bess said, sighing.

"Sure," Deirdre snorted.

Did Sarah Hackett squeeze my hand when I was in the bed, and set the book out where I'd see it? Did she help us out of the burning building? I wondered.

"Thanks, Sarah," I whispered, just in case.

Was that a puff of cold air against my cheek?

THE END

visitor from beyond

"**O**kay, you guys, please tell me what Deirdre said," I asked George and Bess as the sun sparkled on the dew beneath our running shoes. George, Bess, and I had decided that we needed more exercise, so we'd started getting up early, throwing on our sweats, and taking a jog through various picturesque sections of River Heights. Today was Monday, the day we usually jogged around the university sculpture garden for our early morning cardio routine. But what George said next practically gave me a heart attack!

"Don't freak, but Deirdre insists that you're engaged to some redheaded guy who lives in Trib Falls."

"*Engaged?*" I semishrieked. It was hard to do more than that as we huffed and puffed along the footpath winding among stately elms, Greek statues, colorful cubes, and black metal bloblike people who looked like they were whispering secrets to one another. Maybe about my "engagement."

"I heard it from Charlie Adams," George informed me. "For the record, Charlie was happy for you in a sad, now-she'll-never-love-me kind of way."

"I hope Deirdre has been working out," I huffed. "Because she'd better start running. . . ."

The cousins both chuckled as we reached the outskirts of the garden, guarded by a plaster statue of a Greek goddess holding a book and half of a rectangular-shaped lantern. At some point the other half of the lantern had broken off. It was the oldest sculpture on campus; some said she was Athena, the goddess of wisdom; but over time, she got the nickname "Studentia," and it was said that she was looking for the library. Right now I hoped she was on the lookout for Deirdre.

Behind Studentia, there was a large stand of very old pines, seemingly held back from invading the university grounds by a tumbled-down brick wall. The mortar had crumbled long ago—before I was born, anyway. Now and then the university talked about repairing the wall, but no one ever got around to it. We only counted our sculpture garden jog as complete if we touched the wall, so I bounded over, gave the topmost brick a tap, and turned back around. George and Bess did the same.

"Look, speaking of true love, there's Ned, dead ahead," Bess grunted, as we headed back to our start point—the stairs leading to the ivy-covered administration building. "And here *we* are, all gross and sweaty."

Despite my intense irritation with Deirdre, George and I both had to laugh. We might be all gross and sweaty, but Bess sure wasn't. Her blond hair was pulled back in a sleek ponytail and if anything, the pink in her cheeks emphasized the startling blueness of her eyes. Bess was just one of those people who always looked fresh and picture-perfect.

I turned my attention to Ned, who was standing beside the stairs. Brown hair tossed by the wind, brown eyes sparking with good humor, he was collegiate-cute today, in a black jacket and jeans. A short, thin girl with a heart-shaped face that was framed by black hair shifted her weight and studied the ground. She was bundled up in a jacket, jeans, and turtleneck, but she was hunched over as if she were still very cold.

"Good morning," Ned called out, giving us a wave as we approached. "Fancy meeting you here on sculpture garden day."

"Listen. About what Deirdre said . . ." I began, then realized the girl was with him, and I smiled at her. "Hi."

"This is Emily Baker. She's transferring here for a semester on an exchange program with her university in New York," Ned said. "She came to check on her transcripts, but the office doesn't open until nine."

I glanced down at the face of my cell phone. It was eight forty-nine. She had only eleven minutes to go.

"Hi. I'm Nancy," I said. "And these are my partners in crime, George and Bess."

Emily jerked as if I had said something weird. Her eyes widened slightly, and then she looked back down at the ground.

"Hi," she said, in a low, shy voice. Then she glanced up at Ned and mumbled, "Thanks for showing me the office. I'll come back later."

"No problem," Ned replied . . . to her retreating back. She was already walking away as fast as humanly possible without breaking into a run. Her shoulders were pulled tight and her head was down, her hands stuffed into her pockets.

"Wow, talk about shy," Bess said. "It's almost like she's afraid of us."

"Yes," I said, watching her dart around the corner of the building. Or afraid of something else.

"Maybe she'd like to go running," George said, as she placed her hands on her knees and bent over, taking deep breaths. Her short, dark hair brushed around her chin. "I'm sure we would go a lot faster."

"Okay, here's the deal," I said to Ned, resuming my original topic. "Brandon Hawkins was just a client. He hired me to find Lucybelle. Lucybelle is his beagle. I found her. And that is *all*."

"Oh, you're talking about that engagement thing." Ned quirked a brow at me. "You didn't think I'd actually believe that wild rumor?"

"A rumor that Deirdre Shannon started," George piped up as she straightened. Deirdre has had her eye on Ned for a bazillion years. We all knew it—Ned did too—but I suspected that George mentioned her name to remind him that Deirdre was not to be trusted.

"I wouldn't have believed it if *you* started it," Ned told George, giving me an affectionate hug. I hugged back . . . even if I was all gross and sweaty.

"Deirdre has always been such a gossip. She used to spread all kinds of stories in high school," George went on, stretching out her right calf muscle. "She hurt a lot of people."

I gazed off in the direction where Emily Baker had practically fled from us, wondering if anyone had hurt her. She seemed very fragile and vulnerable. What was her story?

"Not to worry," Ned said firmly. "Ned and Nancy are as solid as a brick wall."

"I hope you don't mean the brick wall behind Studentia," I said, giving him a mock-stern look.

"Not that wall," he agreed. "It's definitely a few bricks short. Like Deirdre's gossip-flop."

"Gossip-flop. I like that. You should write for a living," I told him. That was a little joke. Ned worked part-time for his dad at the *River Heights Bugle*, our local newspaper, which his dad owned.

"Speaking of writing, I have a deadline on a story. I'll see you later."

He kissed my cheek and gave the cousins a wave.

For the next week or so, I thought about checking in with Emily Baker to see how she was doing. I had pretty much decided that her total freak-out was probably new-school, new-town jitters. But we didn't know each other, and I figured she'd have made some friends in her classes by now who might help her feel more at home.

Still, I couldn't shake the feeling that there was something more to Emily's anxiety than new-student-hood. When you've been doing detective work as long as I have, you develop a second sense about when things don't quite fit. I didn't want to invade her privacy, but I did conduct a simple online search of her name. There were a lot of Emily Bakers on the Web, but I found "my" Emily Baker on a roster for a class at the university. She was enrolled in "Gothic Literature: Spooks, Phantoms, and Specters." Wow, an entire class about ghosts! Maybe I would take it sometime. I love a good ghost story almost as much as I love mysteries.

Then one evening, as I passed the storefront window of Mugged, our local coffeehouse, I saw her sitting by herself at a circular varnished wood table reading a book. On impulse, I went inside.

Her eyes flicked up apprehensively as the bell on the door tinkled. There were rings under her eyes, and when she saw that it was just me, her shoulders slumped slightly as if she'd been holding her breath.

I smiled at her and crossed the busy room, which was filled with the fragrant odors of coffee and chai tea. Amid the background chatter, the espresso machine was noisily steaming and hissing. There were some papers beside Emily's white coffee cup. The topmost one was a rental agreement.

"Hi," I said, nearing her table. "How's it going?"

She shrugged. "Fine." She followed my gaze to the documents beside her cup. "I rented an apartment near campus today. I didn't want to stay in student housing. Too much partying."

"Do you need help moving?" I asked her. "I'd be happy to help."

"No," she said quickly. "I'm fine."

"Well, if you change your mind, here's my phone number," I told her. I reached into my pocket and pulled out a piece of paper to write my number down on.

"Thanks," she said, setting it on top of her papers without looking at it. Her hand was shaking. I glanced as casually as I could at the book she was reading. The title was listed at the top of the page. It was *Lost Ghosts: How to Find Deceased Family Members . . . and Just About Anyone Else.*

"This is for a class," she told me, snapping the book shut. Then she picked up her coffee cup and took a sip.

"It looks fascinating," I ventured.

She didn't answer. I stood beside her chair,

trying to think of something to say to set her at ease. She set down her cup and kept her attention on her book.

"If you change your mind about my being able to help you, please don't hesitate to call," I said.

I saw Andi Thompson across the way, who did a lot of volunteering at Rags 2 Riches, the thrift store, and gave her a wave. She waved back.

"Help," Emily said. "With moving, you mean."

"Or anything," I replied, turning around to face her. "Seriously." I decided to be a little more direct. "I'm kind of known around town as an amateur detective. I help people. People with problems."

Her eyes grew enormous. Judging by her reaction, I may as well have told her I was an axe murderer. I regretted being so blunt as I watched her eyelids flicker and a blank, protective expression pass over her features.

"I don't have any problems," she replied.

And that was that.

Emily had been in town for about two weeks when I met Ned at the *Bugle* offices. It was a Friday night, and we were going to go to the movies. As he shut down his workstation computer, he told me that the historical archives department of the university library had reported a theft. The only item taken was a scrapbook of life in River Heights during the thirties and forties, put together by a society matron named Grace Horton.

"Why would anyone take an old scrapbook?" I asked him. Then I flashed on the title of the book Emily had been reading in Mugged: *Lost Ghosts*. Maybe someone with an interest in researching the past would be tempted . . .

When I told Ned about it, he made a face.

"You don't think Emily stole the scrapbook, do you?" he asked. "Why would she? She's a university student. She could just ask to look through it in the archives room."

I gave my head a shake. "Maybe she wanted to examine something more closely. She couldn't exactly pry an old picture off a page in the archive room to see if anything was written on the back— like a name or a date." I frowned. "And speaking of prying, I'm going to dig a little deeper."

The next morning, I went to the archives room at the university library to talk to Ms. Falk, the librarian. She told me that a lot of students were using the archives for history projects. I described Emily and she shook her head.

"I don't remember seeing her. But I was in my

office on a long phone call. I can't see the stacks from there. The thief must have taken the scrapbook while I was on that call." She rubbed her forehead anxiously. "That scrapbook is irreplaceable. As soon as we get some more funding, I'm going to scan everything in."

"I'll try to get the scrapbook back for you," I promised her.

"If anyone can, it'll be you, Nancy," she replied, smiling weakly.

Next, I went to the public library to see if they had a copy of *Lost Ghosts*. Our branch didn't, but the librarian ordered it for me via library loan and promised to call me when it arrived.

Then I called Luther Eldredge, who knows tons about local history, and got his permission to stop by for a chat. I headed on over just as it began to get dark. Autumn leaves danced along the side of the road. From my angle, I could see the thick woods pressing in on the university and I thought I saw a flash of white moving through them. Maybe it was a deer.

Or Studentia, searching for the library, I thought. Or maybe she's after the scrapbook too. Even though I smiled at my own joke, I felt a little spooked. It was that kind of dark, wild autumn night.

I felt a little sense of relief as I walked up to Mr. Eldredge's house with its warm, glowing porch light. He was waiting for me, and urged me to come inside to get out of the cold. His small living room was crammed with books and a few photographs of the family he had lost that terrible day of the car accident. He had made us some tea, and he handed me a cup as I sat down on his sofa and relayed what Ms. Falk had told me.

"I hope I didn't have anything to do with the theft." He stirred his tea and set the spoon down on his saucer. "A couple of days ago I had a visitor, a young girl, who said her name was Eleanor Brown. Very shy and uncertain. Pretty, heart-shaped face."

That sounds like Emily Baker, I thought. "Are you sure she said she was Eleanor Brown?"

"I'm sure she said it, but I'm not sure it was true," he replied with a wry grin, almost as if he had read my mind. "She stumbled over it as if she was making it up on the spot. She told me she was taking a class at the university about how to do historical research. One of her professors suggested she come to me. She was interested in missing-persons cases during the 1940s. I asked her a few questions of my own, and I realized she was looking into the Mary Reaves case."

"Mary Reaves?" I asked.

His wry grin became a wistful smile as he leaned against the back of his sofa, the tea wafting toward his face and tingeing his glasses with mist.

"The disappearance of Mary Reaves is one of the most intriguing unsolved mysteries in River Heights history," he informed me. "Mary Reaves came to town in the fall of 1941. She caused quite a stir. She was beautiful—dark hair, dark eyes—and very glamorous. Half the men in town were in love with her and all the society ladies invited her to parties.

"But she never returned the favor—never threw a party, never had so much as lunch with anyone. People felt snubbed. Rumors began to circulate. The one that stuck was that she was a Nazi spy. In fact, she's listed as a probable German agent in a couple of books about the history of espionage."

"A spy!" I cried.

He chuckled. "Well, I don't think she was. But she was definitely up to something. Mary Reaves wasn't her real name. She made it up. That identity completely dead-ends here in River Heights." He raised a brow and paused dramatically. "However, she did disappear the same day Hans Von

Thurman did, and I think she left with him."

"Hans Von Thurman," I said, thinking hard. "That name rings a bell."

As if on cue, my cell phone rang. It was Ned. "There's been a burglary," he told me. "At the Historical Society. I'm on my way over to cover it for the *Bugle*."

"I'll meet you there," I said breathlessly. I turned to Mr. Eldredge. "May I come back later and continue this discussion?"

"Of course. I'm not going anywhere," he replied.

He showed me to the door. I jumped into my hybrid and drove over to the Historical Society, which was located in a beautiful old Victorian mansion on River Street. There was a police car in the parking lot, and I could see Officer Rees of the River Heights PD through the bay window.

Outside on the porch, Ned was interviewing petite, dark-haired Dora Gutierrez, who worked at the Historical Society. Ned brightened when he saw me and waved me over with his notepad. I had known Dora for ages, and she, too, smiled as I approached.

"It looks like the janitorial service forgot to lock the office door and set the alarm," Ned informed me. "Even though the owner is insisting that they didn't. So someone came inside and grabbed the nearest thing. It was a crime of opportunity, nothing premeditated."

Nevertheless, I pulled out my clue notebook and clicked on my pen. A good detective collects the data first, and makes judgments about its usefulness later.

"Was anything taken?" I asked Dora.

She shrugged. "So far, it looks like just a Japanese puzzle box."

My hand hovered over my notepad. "You mean a box holding the pieces of a jigsaw puzzle?"

"No." Dora mimicked holding a box. "You have to slide open different little doors and lids in a specific sequence. Once you figure out the order, you reach a little 'secret compartment.' It's big enough to store a small object like a box of matches, something like that."

Secret compartment! Like a spy would use?

"Was there anything in the secret compartment of your puzzle box?" I asked her. "Something someone might want?"

She shook her head. "It was empty. There might have been something inside it when we first received it, but that was before my time. It's not very valuable. Maybe it was just kids."

"I'll do my best to get it back," I promised her.

"Thank you, Nancy," she replied, glancing through the bay window. "I need to go back inside to talk with Officer Rees." She smiled at us both and headed for the front door.

I turned to Ned. "Are there any suspects?"

"None so far," he replied as we walked along the porch together. "Officer Rees said he'd call me later if there was anything to report." He scrunched up his face. "Sorry to call you over here for a little misdemeanor. I thought it was going to be something bigger."

"I'm glad that it was such a such a little mis-demeanor. And equally glad that you called," I assured him. "Thanks to Mr. Eldredge, I may have a potential lead on the scrapbook theft." I tapped my clue notebook. "For all I know, the puzzle box may be connected."

"So your 'mystery-dar' is on red alert. I was wondering why you were looking so flushed," he teased me.

"It's the chilly air," I retorted, but we both knew he was right.

When we got back to the *Bugle* offices, I ran down what Mr. Eldredge had told me about "Eleanor

Brown" and about Mary Reaves's disappearance.

"He also mentioned a man named Hans Von Thurman," I finished. "You know, Ned, that name sounds familiar but I can't figure out why."

Ned's lips parted and his brows shot up. "What did he say about Von Thurman?"

"Actually," I replied, "he didn't get a chance to say much of anything. You called right then and I left to go to the Historical Society. Why?"

"This will set your 'mystery-dar' on super-red alert." He led me over to his desktop computer, leaned over the chair, and typed in some commands. Then he gestured for me to take a look at the screen. It was a mock-up of a page of the *Bugle*.

LEGENDARY BANK ROBBER DIES
OLD MYSTERY STILL GOES UNSOLVED

Hans Von Thurman, head of a gang that dug a tunnel and blasted open the vault of the First Bank of River Heights on January 17, 1942, has died. Although his exact age could not be determined, he was estimated to be at least ninety years old. The gang stole nearly two hundred pounds of gold, in the form of gold bars, today worth approximately two million dollars. Von Thurman passed away in the infirmary of

the Camarillo State Penitentiary in Camarillo,
California, where he was serving a life sentence
for a string of serious crimes committed in Los
Angeles in March of 1942, just two months
after the River Heights burglary.

On his deathbed, he told an unnamed source,
"Once I'm dead, I'll be free at last to get that
gold. No jail can hold the great Hans Von Thur-
man."

Von Thurman fell into a coma soon after. He
never regained consciousness.

Von Thurman was the last surviving mem-
ber of the notorious Von Thurman Gang, who
robbed banks and grocery stores all over the Mid-
west from 1938 until their capture and arrest
in 1942. In their trials for the robbery, the Von
Thurman gang members described Von Thurman
as an immortal magician who could escape from
any prison "including the grave." He promised
his followers vast wealth and supernatural pro-
tection from their enemies if they would obey his
every command.

Beside the article was a blurry black-and-white
photograph captioned HANS VON THURMAN. Staring back at me was a young man with hollow
cheeks, tight lips, and a long, hooked nose. His

pale eyes seemed to widen as I studied them, and there was something about their piercing, intense gaze that made it difficult to turn away. I felt a chill run down my spine. I broke the spell by blinking my eyes and ticking my glance at Ned.

"Did you feel it too?" Ned asked me. "Some kind of pull?"

I nodded and rubbed my arms. "Brrrr."

Nick scrolled down the screen. "The article goes on to say that they loaded the gold into carts and wheeled it to Von Thurman's car. They were supposed to meet in Trib Falls—where your fiancé lives—but Von Thurman didn't show."

"Lucybelle. Beagle." I gritted my teeth. Ned just smiled.

"The police *did* show, though. Still, all his men initially believed Von Thurman had received a supernatural warning to stay away. They assumed he would break them out of jail with his magic powers and share the gold."

"He must have chosen them for their brains," I observed. "Or lack thereof."

"My thought as well," Ned said. "If you can believe it, after a few months in jail only one of them, a guy named Lester Clancy, denounced Von Thurman as a con man. He told a guard he wanted to talk about another crime Von Thurman had committed, but he died before he had the chance."

"Lester Clancy died?" I echoed. "How?"

"Another prisoner attacked him."

"Another crime. Another mystery. I wonder what Clancy was going to reveal," I mused.

"That's not all," Ned continued. "Ten years ago, another gang member, Lefty Vernia, asked to see the jail chaplain so he could get something off his chest. A visit was arranged for the following day, but Lefty died that night."

I raised my brows. "Was he also attacked?"

"No. He just died. No apparent cause of death."

"Creepy," I said, making a show of shivering. I could feel the wheels of my brain turning as I silently reread the article. "The gold's never been recovered?"

"No. I *knew* that would unleash your inner detective," he told me, his grin broadening into a wide smile.

The wheels kept turning like a combination lock. Then they clicked into place and I had an *aha!* moment—the best kind of moment for a detective to have. "Ned," I said excitedly, "maybe that's why Emily Baker came to River Heights. And why she's so jumpy."

"To find the gold?" he asked.

"Mary Reaves must be the key," I replied, nodding. "And Emily must know it. If Emily wouldn't even give Mr. Eldredge her real name, she must be doing something she doesn't want anyone else to know about." I cocked my head at him and asked with a sly smile, "Do you want to go with me to do a follow-up with Mr. Eldredge?"

He smiled back and powered down his computer. "Of course."

We were back at Mr. Eldredge's in less than twenty minutes. The news of Hans Von Thurman's death intrigued him, and he, Ned, and I agreed it was beyond coincidental that "Eleanor Brown" had come to inquire about Mary Reaves just days before the "immortal magician" died.

"Maybe Von Thurman and Eleanor/Emily knew each other," I suggested. "If he realized he was dying, he could have given her some clues about where the gold is hidden. Then she hurried here as fast as she could. I imagine there will be other treasure hunters once the *Bugle* runs the story."

"That's true," Ned agreed, as Mr. Eldredge set down three cups of tea. "It's coming out on Monday."

I had another *aha!* moment. "Do you think Emily could be related to Hans Von Thurman or Mary Reaves? If Von Thurman and Mary ran away together . . ." I trailed off. "Maybe she's their great-granddaughter." I turned to Mr. Eldredge. "You mentioned having some books with pictures of Mary Reaves in them?"

"Yes. I'll go get them." He rose and left the room.

"But why would he give her *clues* if he could just tell her where it was?" I continued, talking mostly to myself. I do that when I'm working on a case—get so focused I kind of forget about my surroundings and concentrate on the mystery. "Did he have to be careful because he was in jail? Was it some kind of test to see if she was smart enough to figure out his puzzle? Puzzle! Ned!"

In my excitement, I jerked on his sleeve and he nearly spilled his tea. "The puzzle box! Von Thurman may have told her there was some sort of clue inside."

Ned paused. "I just can't picture her waltzing in and taking something. She was afraid of her own shadow."

"Or so it appeared," I replied. "Appearances can be deceiving."

"Here we go," Mr. Eldredge announced, walking back into the room. He was balancing an opened leather-bound book on top of another one. "And here she is."

Nick and I both peered at a picture of a woman with dark hair in a soft, shoulder-length cut and a suit with sharp shoulder pads and a pleated skirt standing in front of a brick wall. There was a caption beneath it: *Mary Reaves, River Heights, December 1941*. A shadow was cast across her face, obscuring most of her features. There was some kind of boxy object poking into the left side of the frame.

"'The reclusive Mary Reaves,'" I read. "'Was she a spy, fortune hunter, or the moll of a gangster? A brief search was conducted after her disappearance, but she was never seen again.'"

"What's that?" Nick asked, pointing to the object.

"I don't know," Mr. Eldredge said. "It looks like a box."

"Half of a puzzle box?" I mused. "I wish that shadow wasn't covering her face. Let's check the other book."

Mr. Eldredge flipped it open. The picture was nearly identical, except it was taken from a different angle. So they were two off the same roll of film. She was standing in front of the brick wall, but the box—or whatever it was—was missing from the frame.

It was much easier to see her features in the second picture. Her face was decidedly heart-shaped, and her eyes were as dark and deep-set as Emily Baker's.

"She looks like the girl who came to see me," Mr. Eldredge confirmed.

"Bingo," Ned said, as I flipped to the front of the book, looking to see if there were any photo credits for the pictures. I didn't see any.

"Will you tell me if she comes to see you again?" I asked. "And may I take these books with me?"

He nodded. "Yes. If you solve any part of this mystery, Nancy Drew, please let me know."

"I will," I promised. Of course, I hoped to solve all of it.

The next morning dawned cold and drizzly. As I dressed in my sweats and running shoes, I checked my e-mail. Ned had sent me the final draft of his story, complete with the picture of Hans Von Thurman. Then Bess called, pleading to be spared from our run because of the threat of rain.

"Let's meet at Mugged instead," she suggested. "We can speed up our heart rates with caffeine."

I decided to print out Nick's story so I could read it at the coffee shop. Then I climbed in my hybrid and drove off, peering through the windshield at the gathering storm clouds. I had driven a few blocks when I saw a River Heights PD car parked outside Rags 2 Riches. The thrift store's interior lights were on, even though the store wouldn't open for another two hours. I slowed, curious, when my cell phone ringtone trilled.

"Nancy?" It was Emily Baker. Her voice was barely a whisper. "Nancy, can you meet me?"

"Yes, of course," I replied, forcing myself to stay calm.

"Th-thank you," she stammered. "I'm at Mugged."

"I'm on my way there now," I said. "Are you okay?"

"I-I don't know," she replied. "I mean, yes, I'm okay. But I think someone's been following me."

I glanced over at the police car, giving a thought to asking for help, but if she was inside Mugged, she was safe for the moment.

"Please hurry," she said. "I'm really s-scared."

"I'll be there in five minutes," I informed her. "Sit tight."

★★★★

I stayed on the phone with Emily. As I got out of my car and hurried toward the coffeehouse, I waved my arm so that she could see me. Then I darted inside, looking around for her.

"I'm in the corner," she informed me over the phone. "The dark one."

Sure enough, Emily sat hunched in one of two overstuffed chairs facing each other in the darkest corner of Mugged. A hanging pot of ivy partially obscured the left side of her face, reminding me of the first picture of Mary Reaves that I had seen. A backpack sat at her feet.

I forced myself to remain calm as I took the chair across from her. A small table separated us.

"Hi," I said. "What can I do for you?"

She clutched her hands in her lap. "You said you help people. . . ."

"I do," I replied.

She stared down at her fingernails, coated with black polish, for a few seconds. I put down my purse, my phone, and the printout of Ned's article. Then she caught her breath and swallowed hard. Her large eyes grew larger as she pointed at the picture of Hans Von Thurman.

"That's him," she said. "That's the man who's following me."

★★★★

I ordered some chai tea for both of us while Emily read Ned's story about Von Thurman. When she finished, she was so frightened she was practically in tears. Without a word, she pointed to the third paragraph on the second page—something Ned had added in his final draft, that I hadn't yet read:

Shortly after the trials of Von Thurman's six accomplices, newspapers all over the country began receiving reports of "Hans sightings." A bush pilot in Fairbanks, Alaska, claimed to have seen him walking across an ice field surrounded by silent wolves. A woman in New Orleans insisted he had danced beside her in a voodoo ceremony.

Of course, none of these sightings was accurate, as Von Thurman was in custody in Los Angeles by then. When informed of the sightings, Von Thurman's followers insisted that this was proof that he was a magician, as he claimed.

"I saw him early this morning," Emily told me. "I couldn't sleep, so I got up and walked to my back window. And I swear I saw him underneath the streetlight, staring up at me."

"Or you saw someone who looks like him," I replied cautiously. "Maybe a relative, looking for the gold he left behind." I took a little breath, wondering how she would react to my statement.

She exhaled slowly and nodded as if to herself. "So you know," she said.

Know what? I wanted to ask, but I kept quiet. Sometimes people fill in the blanks for me without realizing what they're doing.

But not Emily Baker. We sat in silence, sipping tea. Emily read the article through again and gazed up at me through her lashes.

Then she raised her chin as if she'd come to some sort of decision. "Nancy," she blurted edgily, "would you come back with me to my apartment?"

"Sure," I said. "And if that creep is there, we'll call the police."

"I don't know," she murmured.

"Emily, please, tell me what's going on. I want to help you. I really do."

Then the bell on the front door of Mugged jingled and I heard George call out, "Nancy! Where are you?"

"Oh, no," Emily whispered, reaching for her pack.

I gently put my hand over hers. "Emily, George and Bess are my best friends. They'll do everything they can to help you, just like me."

She caught her lower lip between her teeth. Then George and Bess appeared, George pointing triumphantly at the window. It had begun to rain.

"What did I tell you?" she said. Then she grinned at Emily. "Hey, Emily, how are you? We met a while ago on campus."

"Guys," I said, "Emily and I have to go do something." I nodded encouragingly at her.

"You-you can come too," she told them.

"What is it?" Bess asked. "What are you going to do?"

"Solve a mystery, hopefully," I replied.

Emily, George, Bess, and I piled into my hybrid. Emily had taken the bus to Mugged; it wasn't that far.

She gazed out the window at the blurry landscape, trees and buildings looking ghostlike in the rain. The sound of my windshield wiper blades *tick-tocked* back and forth like a steady heartbeat.

"Over there," Emily said, pointing to a brick apartment building lined with elm trees. "That's where I live."

We piled out, pushing open umbrellas and quickly darting into the dimly lit foyer. Then

Emily led the way up a flight of stairs and down a hall, putting her key in the lock of the third door from the end.

She gazed at me again, as if making absolutely certain that she wanted to let me in.

Then she said, "There are some things I want to show you about my great-aunt, Miriam Ramsey. Only here in River Heights, she went by Mary Reaves."

Miriam Ramsey. Mary Reaves! I wanted to throw up my hands and cry "Woo hoo!" but Emily was still very frightened. While this might be a case to me, it was something scary that was happening in Emily's actual life.

"What are you guys talking about?" George asked.

"Shh, let her talk," Bess said. "Then we'll find out."

Emily pushed open the door. We entered a small but pleasantly furnished one-bedroom apartment. The rain pattered on the roof as she set down her backpack and crossed to a small bookshelf.

"I never met her," Emily said. "There were all kinds of theories about what happened to her. Some people thought she went off with Hans Von Thurman. Others figured that he . . . he killed her. I thought a lot about her. I guess you could say I identify with her. I've always felt close to her, somehow. I can't explain it."

She gestured to a beige sofa. "Please, sit down," she invited George and Bess. I took one of the dinette chairs.

"I wrote a poem about Miriam on my blog," she said. "About a year ago, a man named Rob O'Brien in upstate New York contacted me. He had just inherited the house his father grew up in. He was going through some things in the attic and he came across some letters addressed to his great-uncle, Andrew. Apparently Andrew had been engaged to Miriam Ramsey when she disappeared. When Rob did an online search of Miriam Ramsey's name, my poem popped up."

"What kind of letters?" I asked.

She walked to the bookshelf and bent down. Pushing aside a book titled *Visions From Beyond the Grave,* she picked up a manila envelope. She held it for a moment as if she had one more moment of uncertainty, then pulled open the flap and eased out some pieces of paper. I realized they were photocopies.

She handed them to me, saying, "The last one she wrote is on the top."

I read aloud:

"January 14, 1941

"My darling,

"Please don't be angry with me for writing you. My nerves are stretched to the limit. HVT keeps staring at me as if he knows, but he can't possibly. I've been so very, very careful. I have seen evidence of his terrible hold over people, and while I still can't bring myself to believe he has magical powers, he is terrifying.

"And yet he is so egotistical that he does not doubt my attraction to him, even for a moment. In fact, he willingly took several photographs of me standing in the very place where I suspect he plans to hide the gold. I put the pictures in the puzzle box. I will put the box in the agreed-upon location. If anything happens to me, tell the police where to look."

My heart jumped. So the puzzle box had contained pictures! I thought about the photographs I had seen of "Mary Reaves." Standing in front of a brick wall, with something rectangular to her left . . .

"Keep reading," Bess pleaded.

"This will be my last letter until it's over. Soon we will be married and honeymooning in

Italy. It sounds like such a wonderful dream.
"With all my love,
"Miriam."

"Andrew never heard from her again," Emily said.

"I have the chills," Bess said, rubbing her arms.

"This is the guy she's writing about," I told Bess, handing her the picture from Nick's article. "HVT."

"Yikes." Bess showed it to George. "He looks like a serial killer."

"And here's Miriam," Emily murmured, fishing a small black-and-white photo out of the envelope. It was the same woman who had been identified as Mary Reaves in Mr. Eldredge's books, but she wore a soft dress and her hair was pulled back in a ponytail. I glanced from the photo to Emily and back again.

"I know. I look a lot like her," Emily said.

"Emily, did you find her puzzle box at the Historical Society?" I asked her.

She looked confused. So did Bess and George. "What are you talking about?"

"A puzzle box was taken from the Historical Society last night. Someone also took a scrapbook from the university library." I deliberately avoided using the world "stole" to soften my accusation.

Emily's eyes grew huge. "No, I didn't."

My phone rang, and everyone jumped. It was Ned.

"There's been another puzzle-box theft," he told me.

"Let me guess. Rags 2 Riches. I saw a police car out there earlier today."

"Very good, detective," Ned replied. "And guess what else? This time the perpetrator was caught on tape. Rags 2 Riches has a security camera."

"And he was a dead ringer for Von Thurman," I ventured, then regretted my choice of words as Emily sucked in her breath and balled her fists beneath her chin.

"A relative, obviously. He must be somewhere in River Heights," Nick agreed.

"He's been following Emily Baker, who is the great-grandniece of Mary Reaves," I added. "I'm in Emily's apartment right now. George and Bess are here too."

"I see you've been putting your puzzle pieces together," Ned said, laughing.

"I have," I told him.

Anxiously, Emily gestured for me to get off the phone.

"I've got to go," I told him. "But I'll catch up with you later. Okay, Ned?"

"Okay. But Nancy? Please be careful."

"Of course," I told him.

We hung up. Emily swayed a little and pulled out one of two chairs of a dinette set, plopping down heavily and crossing her hands over her chest.

"There's someone in town who looks like him," I confirmed. "He stole another puzzle box from a thrift store called Rags 2 Riches. That's the second puzzle box he's taken. But Emily, you know he's not actually Hans Von Thurman."

"Okay, you should probably know I'm into, um, ghosts and things," she murmured. "Look for the letter dated 1959."

She gestured to the stack of photocopies I was holding. I paged through them and found the one she meant.

"'This is your last warning. Stop looking into things that don't concern you, or you'll end up like her,'" I read aloud. "'I can make it happen. I have powers you can't even imagine.'" I looked questioningly at Emily.

"Andrew O'Brien didn't stop looking," Emily half-whispered. "Then one day in 1960, when he was walking down a street, a flowerpot fell off a window sill, hit him on the head, and killed him instantly."

"Oh, my God," Bess whispered, turning very pale.

"Bess, please, it was an accident," George said, rolling her eyes. "A tragic accident, but an accident. Right, Emily? No one *threw* the flowerpot?"

"There were no witnesses," Emily insisted. She gave her head a sharp shake. "Maybe this wasn't such a good idea."

She darted forward and took the photocopies out of my hand. Stuffing the papers back in the envelope, she replaced it in the bookcase. A book on the far end of the shelf tumbled onto the floor. Emily was too preoccupied to notice. Bess was closest to it; she bent forward from the couch and picked it up. It was titled *True Ghost Stories.* She looked up at me with a frightened expression and quickly put it back on the shelf.

"Let's think this through," I said. "Hans Von Thurman is dead. He won't care if you find out the truth about Miriam's disappearance. Although I have to say," I added gently, "that it's pretty obvious that he must have killed her."

"He was already in prison for life when he threatened Andrew O'Brien," Emily countered, keeping her back to me.

"Maybe he hoped he'd be paroled, or he actually believed he was going to get out of jail using his magical powers," George argued. "Or he warned Andrew off because he didn't want anyone else to find his loot. But the ghost of Hans Von Thurman would know where the gold was hidden. So if he's come back to River Heights to collect it, why would he be stealing scrapbooks and puzzle boxes in search of clues?"

"Maybe it's like you said. He's trying to collect anything that might reveal where the gold is because he doesn't want anyone else to find it," Emily suggested.

"It's been over seventy years," George pressed. "He'd probably have more luck buying up all the puzzle boxes for sale on the Internet than coming to River Heights and stealing them one by one."

Emily didn't say anything.

"If you believed he could hurt you, why did you come to River Heights?" Bess asked softly, rising and putting a hand on Emily's arm. "Why now? Did you know he was dying?"

Emily opened her mouth to speak, then cast a doubtful glance at George. Maybe George sensed she was pushing too hard. She pantomimed zipping her mouth and tossing away the key, and Emily's face softened a little.

"Please tell us," I said. "We can help you better if we know all the facts."

"I didn't know he was dying, and that's part of the reason I'm so scared," she admitted. "The timing. After Rob and I met, and I read Miriam's letters, I just knew I had to come here and find out what really happened. I dreamed about her. I-I had a tarot card reading and it said I should 'quest for the one who is lost.'"

"We have a good friend who does tarot readings," Bess said. She was talking about Lucia Gonsalvo, who owns the Psychic's Parlor.

Hearing that, Emily looked a little more confident. "I kept dreaming about Miriam. It was like she was begging me to finish what Andrew O'Brien had started. But I didn't know how to go about it, other than to drop out of college or move here for a summer. My parents would have freaked and we're already not on the best of terms.

"Then one day I was going to see my adviser at school, and a brochure fell out of a big wall display about travel opportunities. It was about studying here for a semester," she continued. "I hadn't even realized we had a program with River Heights. It was like a nudge to finally look into it."

"Like a hand from beyond," Bess murmured.

Emily cast down her gaze and she began to pick at her fingernail polish. "Maybe," she whispered.

With a little groan, George spoke up again. "Emily, you're Miriam's descendant. This guy who looks like Von Thurman must be *his* descendant, searching for the gold. That's the only logical explanation."

After a beat, Emily looked more hopeful than doubtful. Maybe George's clearheaded thinking was beginning to get through to her.

"Whatever the details, it's creepy that he's following you around," I cut in. "Why don't you come stay with my dad and me? We have a nice big house and our housekeeper loves to fuss over my friends." I smiled at her warmly, willing her to say yes.

"You should take Nancy up on it," George advised her. "She'll keep you safe *and* I'm willing to bet solve this mystery a lot faster if you're working on the case beside her. *And* you have never tasted chocolate cake like Hannah Gruen's."

"C'mon," I urged.

"You're really nice," Emily said, ducking her head. "You really do like to help people."

"I really do," I replied.

****

There wasn't much to pack. We made short work of it and then we three drove Emily over to our house. I told George and Bess I'd drive them back to Mugged later.

Hannah greeted Emily like a long-lost daughter and told her she needed to put some meat on her bones. She invited George and Bess for lunch, and then we got on my computer. George is a superhacker whose skills have helped me bust tons of cases wide open.

"Let's see . . . Hans Von Thurman . . . I'll go to the prison rolls . . . there he is, long prisoner ID number, now directories . . . Camarillo . . . hmm, look at this. Janet Von Thurman. Checking public records . . ." George grinned. "Bingo. She's his mother. Moved to Camarillo in 1943, no doubt to be near him. She had another son . . . let's see where he lived . . . New Mexico . . . moved also to Camarillo. Married . . ."

"That's amazing," Emily murmured, watching George with undisguised admiration. "I was just about to read the chapter on Internet searches in *Lost Ghosts*. It looked very complicated."

"Once you learn a few tricks, stuff like this is easy," George said modestly.

George kept working. After about an hour,

she pushed back from my desk and gestured to the screen.

"Here's your phantom," she announced.

Emily sucked in her breath. The face of Hans Von Thurman gazed back us in all his pale-eyed, hooked-nosed weirdness. Except he was dressed in a basketball uniform, and the name beneath the picture read JASON VON THURMAN.

"High school picture," George said. "He's eighteen in it. He's twenty now and lives in Camarillo. Hans Von Thurman's great-grandnephew."

"He must have spotted you somewhere and noted your resemblance to your great-aunt and started following you," I told Emily. "Maybe he thinks you know where the gold is. But he's just a flesh-and-blood person."

"With creepy eyes," George added.

"I think I need to sit down," Emily said, perching on the edge of my desk. She glanced at the screen, then looked away. "So his great-uncle murdered my great-aunt."

I took her hand. She felt very cold.

"Let's see if we can find Miriam, and lay to her rest," I said, more quietly.

I called Ned again and asked him to meet me at the newspaper office. I wanted to study the archived issues of the paper on the date of the heist and the days following to see if I could find any clues there. I took Mr. Eldredge's books with me for reference.

Emily stayed at my house while I drove George and Bess back to Mugged to collect their cars. Ned was waiting for me at the *Bugle*, and he smiled happily as I handed him a large slice of Hannah's cake.

"Thanks," he said. Then he hesitated. "You know, you're a very capable person. You've solved some strange cases. . . ."

I raised a brow at him. "But?"

"But I have some qualms about your getting involved in such a dangerous case. I liked the Lucybelle case better."

"Ned." I gave him my patented I-will-not-be-dissuaded expression. "You're sweet, but I'm doing this."

He sighed. "Okay. You'd think I would have learned by now." He gestured to the desktop monitor. "I have the January 17th, 1941, evening edition on the screen, but you can scroll through the database for any date you want. Meanwhile, I'm hitting the staff fridge in the break room for some milk to go with this little slice of heaven."

"Okay," I said. I scanned the headlines that read

BANK ROBBED! GOLD TAKEN! and read the by-now familiar details of the heist. I studied the entire paper, unsure of what I was looking for. I even read the ads, marveling at the low prices and the vintage fashions.

I scrolled to January 18th. The headline was about the apprehension of the Von Thurman gang. I read it carefully, studying all the photographs of the gang members. There were Lester Clancy and Lefty Vernia, both of whom would die before they had a chance to tell what they knew about Hans Von Thurman.

I moved to the next page, and the next. And then I got that funny feeling I sometimes get when I'm on to something. My face tingled and my breathing grew shallow.

On the second-to-last page of January 18th, there was a black-and-white photograph of Studentia, fallen over on her side. A glowering young man in a sweater, tie, and baggy trousers was kneeling beside her, pointing to her lantern. It was broken in half. A boy in a cap beside him was holding the broken piece and showing it to the camera. Another young man in a sweatshirt with RH on it was gesturing to the wall behind her, tumbled down much as it was today.

The headline read DELTA SIGMA TAU BLAMES

"Oh, my gosh," I exclaimed, reading the article. "Athena" had been a gift from Delta Sigma Tau to the university, and they were accusing their traditional rival fraternity of pushing her over the night before. Her lantern had broken in the melee. They also claimed that Delta Delta had destroyed the wall. The other fraternity, Delta Delta, was denying it.

So that was how she got broken, I thought. *And how the wall fell down.*

But even then I knew, deep down, that it wasn't how the statue had fallen over. I flipped through Mr. Eldredge's books to the pictures of Miriam, standing in front of a brick wall—*that* wall—and fumbled in my purse for my magnifying glass. I placed it over the different pictures and compared them. The square object that cast a shadow on her face was Studentia's lantern, fully intact.

"Ned," I said again, "I think I know where the gold is hidden."

"Hmm?" he queried, coming into the room with his container of milk and his mouth full of chocolate cake.

It had begun to rain again as Ned and I piled into my hybrid and drove to campus. At my request, he'd located a shovel in the *Bugle's* storage room.

To avoid being spotted, I parked on the wood-side of the sculpture garden. All we could see were trees, but I knew the statue of Studentia was only about twenty feet in. I always carried a flashlight in my purse—every decent detective does—and Ned grabbed the other one out of my glove compartment.

We opened our umbrellas, but as soon as we reached the thick woods, I realized they'd be useless. I pulled up the hood on my jacket and Ned put on a knitted cap. He gave me a thumbs-up—he's such a trooper—and we shouldered our way through the pouring rain. Lightning flashed against the bobbing tree branches and the trunks vibrated with thunder.

We pushed through a stand of thick pines as another zigzag of lightning illuminated the scene approximately ten feet in front of us. Both of us drew back, staring in astonishment.

There he was, Jason Von Thurman, knee-deep in a hole he was digging behind the wall. He was using a shovel much like ours. A flashlight lay on the ground, and in its glare I saw a dark object in a plastic bag lying on the ground.

Lighting burst through the sky again, illuminating Studentia's profile. She was looking in the opposite direction, as if she were keeping watch.

He kept digging. Occasionally, he'd glance around, but we kept to the shadows where he wouldn't be able to see us. Then I heard his shovel clank against something, and I caught my breath.

He looked left, right, and behind himself, then dropped to his knees and let out a short cheer. With a grunt, he hefted something over his head with both hands and let his head drop back. Lightning danced in the sky, and the thing that he held glinted before he brought it back down to the muddy ground with a thud. A gold bar!

Ned gazed at me, and I at him.

I pulled out my cell phone and dialed the River Heights Police Department. Taking a few quiet steps back among the trees, I softly asked the switchboard to page Chief McGinnis for me. We've successfully worked a lot of cases together, even though the chief doesn't love the fact, and I usually give him all the credit, to stay on his good side. He needed to be here, as soon as possible.

I put the phone on vibrate for his call back, and kept watching.

Suddenly, Jason got to his feet and took a step back. He said, "Oh, Hans. Oh, man."

At the same time, lightning sizzled through the

sky, throwing a beam of light around Studentia's head. And to this day, I swear, I really did see what I saw next: Studentia's head lowered, as if in sorrow.

"*Ned,*" I whispered, as chills ran down my spine and my stomach did a somersault. "*Look.*"

"What?" he whispered back.

With the next flash of lightning, her head was back in its normal position.

My phone vibrated. I walked backward into the woods and told Chief McGinnis what was going on.

"I'll be there in ten minutes," he told me.

We watched Jason dig while we waited. He was far more nervous, and he sped up until he was panting from the effort. I was trembling, and not just from the cold. I kept looking from Jason to the statue and back again. Ned slipped his hand in mine as Jason placed something white on the ground, and I knew it was a bone. Jason had found Miriam Ramsey.

I called Emily and told her as gently as I could.

Chief McGinnis was as good as his word; he showed up with three officers. They circled Jason soundlessly. They aimed their flashlights at his face, and told him to freeze. He whirled around and stared straight at me. I knew he couldn't see past the glare of the lights, but his wild, pale eyes bore into me, and I felt another quiver down my spine.

And then . . . I thought I saw the silhouette of another Jason, standing off to the right, beyond the ring of flashlights. I caught my breath, blinked . . . and he was gone.

We all met up at the River Heights PD headquarters, a haven against the rain and the strange things I had seen in the graveyard. I still smelled the mud from the unmarked grave Jason Von Thurman had opened after seventy long years. In the back room, someone had microwaved some popcorn.

"We've recovered all the gold," Chief McGinnis informed Ned, Emily, my dad, and me, as Jason Von Thurman shivered beneath a blanket while an officer inputted his arrest report. They really didn't have much on him—breaking and entering, petty theft, and defacement of a university document. He confessed that he had the scrapbook; he and the chief would be leaving in a few minutes to collect it and all his other things at Jason's cheap motel in Muskoka Valley.

"And you found Miriam," Emily said softly. She cocked her head at Jason. "You must have stolen the right puzzle box."

Looking guilty and uneasy, he nodded.

"How did you know to look for it?" I asked him.

"I always knew the family story of why Uncle Hans was in jail," he began. "I visited him a lot, but he never talked about the gold he had left behind in River Heights.

"But that was before he got sick. The last time I went to visit him, he was half out of his mind on painkillers. He started raving about his gold. He said he had buried the gold under 'the statue.' He also said there were pictures of the statue in a puzzle box. Miriam Ramsey had given it to someone for safekeeping, and he didn't know where it was."

"I wonder who had it," I said. "And why they didn't give it to the police."

"Another mystery," my dad said, with a lop-sided grin at me.

Jason sighed and shook his head. "You have no idea how many statues there are in River Heights. Or puzzle boxes."

He gazed at Emily. "I didn't mean to scare you," he told her. "I didn't realize you had seen me following you. I'm not very good at this stuff."

He took a breath. "And I'm sorry about your aunt. I suspected Uncle Hans had killed her and buried her with the gold. But I didn't know for sure until I found, until . . ." He trailed off, looking stricken. "Until tonight," he finished.

I turned to Chief McGinnis. "I know they're evidence, but may I please see the pictures that were in the puzzle box?"

He pursed his lips. Finally he sighed and nodded.

"Wear gloves," he warned.

I did as Chief McGinnis asked, and slipped on blue latex gloves. Then I crossed to the desk with the object I had seen in the rain, which turned out to be the puzzle box wrapped in a protective plastic bag. I pulled it out, examining the faded sides painted with pictures of cranes for a moment before I saw the first piece I needed to slide forward, in order to move the next piece; and so on. I worked it until I saw a tiny red drawer pull.

I tugged on it, and a small lid slid open, revealing what appeared to be a business card. Confused, I picked it up.

"This says, 'Thank you for your purchase. The money you have spent at Rags 2 Riches will be donated to several worthy causes.'" I looked at Jason. "Where are the pictures?"

"What are you talking about?" he demanded, rising from his chair. No one stopped him as he came up beside me. "I've never seen that card before. There were two photographs of Miriam Ramsey standing in front of that statue." He picked up the puzzle box and shook it.

He put down the box and gazed accusingly at me with those wild Von Thurman eyes. "What did you do with them?"

"Nothing," I told him honestly.

No one ever saw the pictures Jason claimed to have seen. And no one else saw the statue of Studentia lower her head. To this day, Emily believes that forces from beyond the grave led Jason and me to Miriam's unmarked grave that cold, rainy night.

Miriam lies in a cemetery in New York now, next to her loving fiancé, Andrew.

I got a letter from Emily yesterday:

Dear Nancy,
Thank you so much for sharing your reward money from the bank with me. Like I said, you didn't need to do it. I'm going to use it to continue my college education. Please say hi to George and Bess. I'm looking forward to your visit this summer.
—Emily

At Emily's urging, all charges against Jason Von Thurman were dropped. The last thing I heard, a Hollywood producer was interested in telling his story.

I gave most of the reward to Ms. Falk as a donation for her document-scanning project. But I saved some money for a dozen red roses, and placed them on the spot where Miriam Ramsey had lain for over seventy years.

As I arranged the ribbons over the ground, I felt someone staring at me, and quickly looked around. There was no one there; but out of the corner of my eye, I thought I saw a flash of white. . . .

. . . and perhaps a little smile, on Studentia's face.

THE END

carnival of fear

"Halloween and Cutter Brothers Funland, together again," my dad said, as we drove past the darkened amusement park. I was taking him to the airport; he had an important meeting in Washington, DC.

From the window of my hybrid, I could see the silhouette of the Ferris wheel against the glowing, full moon, and the twists and turns of the brand-new roller coaster. Too much of the old wooden structure had rotted away to refurbish it. I had heard that some of the gargoyle statues and wax figures in the fun house were original, though, and I was looking forward to seeing them.

"I can remember wishing I was old enough to ride the Spinner," my dad said. "Of course, that wish never came true. I suppose I should count my lucky stars."

I shivered. What if my dad had ridden the Spinner the night it spun out of control, killing pretty teenager Genevieve Martine?

181

The death of Genie Martine was a River Heights legend. For decades, kids had dared each other to sneak onto the deserted grounds of Funland and stand in the spot where the ghost of Genie was said to appear, doomed to haunt the place where she died until the end of time.

You were supposed to stay perfectly still, close your eyes, and call her name five times: "Genie, Genie, Genie, Genie, Genie . . ." Then you might be able to hear her crying, mourning her own tragic end. We'd all done it—George, Bess, Ned, me, and even Deirdre Shannon—but now, listening to my dad, who had been a little boy when the tragedy had occurred, I felt bad. We had treated it like a game. But a girl my age had actually died.

"They didn't put the Spinner back in," I told him. "There's a fun house where it used to be."

"That's probably a good idea," he replied.

There was a lot of controversy surrounding the reopening of Funland. Some people thought it was tasteless, and that if anything was to be done with the property, it ought to be something like a municipal park. Other people still fondly remembered the old tradition of riding the roller coaster on Halloween night in full costume and declared that Funland was a living piece of River

Heights history and should be welcomed back.

All I knew was that George's and Bess's twelve-year-old siblings, Maggie and Scott, were waiting for my return from the airport. The new owners of Funland had put in a pumpkin patch, and we were all going to go to Funland to get our Halloween pumpkins and go on a few rides. Ned would meet us there.

I kissed my dad good-bye at the airport, then drove back to Bess's house, where the two twelve-year-olds were pacing anxiously. George, Bess, Scott, Maggie, and I piled into my hybrid and before we knew it, we were parking in the Funland lot.

They had saved the old sign, a wooden arch that spanned a broad walkway leading up to the ticket booths. CUTTER BROTHERS FUNLAND was spelled out in large light bulbs. The two younger cousins ran on ahead, yelling at us to hurry up.

"Welcome to Funland," said the woman in the ticket booth. She wore her long gray hair in braids and a red jacket embroidered with FUN-LAND in white. "We sell individual tickets or wristbands. The wristbands will get you into the pumpkin patch, too."

"Then we have to have wristbands, of course,"

I said. Scott and Maggie jumped up and down and cheered.

"Five wristbands," the woman said. She opened a drawer.

"Have you seen the ghost of Genie Martine?" Scott asked her.

"Why, yes, I have," the woman replied, looking at him with a dead serious expression on her face. "Every night, she walks through the park, making sure everyone has gone home to sleep snug in their beds."

Scott flashed her a crooked don't-hand-me-that, I-am-practically-a-teenager grin. The woman gave me a little wink as she snapped our neon green wristbands on to our left wrists. Then we walked through a gate painted with a huge clown face and voilà! we were inside the new and improved Funland.

"What shall we do first?" I asked.

"Roller coaster!" Scott shouted. "It's supposed to be so fast it makes you barf!"

"There's something to look forward to," George deadpanned.

As the kids barreled on ahead, I pulled out my phone and checked in with Ned. He was already inside Funland, and he said he'd meet us at the entrance to the coaster.

The roller coaster was of the enormous gut-wrenching loop-de-loop terror-inducing variety, shooting straight up into the sky, then plummeting nearly straight down—with the riders upside down. It looked so extreme I actually burst out laughing.

"You'd think they'd show a little restraint, given their history," George ventured.

Then I saw Ned, with his hands in the pockets of this great bomber jacket he had bought on one of our day trips to Chicago . . . listening and nodding to Deirdre, of all people, who seemed to be having trouble with her mouth. As in, it wouldn't close.

Don't get me wrong. I know that Nick cannot be lured away. My irritation stemmed more from the fact that she was there at all, than that she was talking to my boyfriend.

I stepped right up and smiled pleasantly at both of them.

"Oh, hi, Nancy," Deirdre said, sweet as Hannah's chocolate cake. "I was just showing Ned my cool new earrings. Belle Cutter, the owner of Funland, gave them to my father in thanks for all the legal work he did for her. In addition to free passes for life." Deirdre Shannon's father was a lawyer, like mine. Well, actually, not like mine.

My father prided himself on his unshakable sense of ethics. Mr. Shannon, Esquire, was not above cutting a few moral corners to win a case.

Shady lawyer father or not, I had to admit that Deirdre's earrings were awfully interesting. They were little dolls with cherubic faces, wearing headdresses and little circus tutus of real feathers. When Deirdre shook her head, they bobbed and danced.

"They're called Kewpie dolls," Deirdre said. "They were all the rage back when Funland first opened. The carnival booths gave away Kewpie-doll earrings, Kewpie-doll pins, and even actual Kewpie dolls as game prizes. These are vintage."

Before I could say anything, she popped open her purse and pulled out a tube of lip gloss. It was one of those incredibly expensive brands that I could never afford. I guessed she was showing off for my benefit—or maybe she was just hoping that Ned would stare at her glossy bee-sting mouth.

"You guys! Let's *go*!" Scott said, ready to bolt for the coaster line.

"No way," George said. "I'm too young to die. But someone should ride with Scott and Maggie."

Bess grimaced. "I don't want to die either."

"Speaking of dying," said a voice behind me. It was Charlie Adams. Charlie drove the emergency truck for Carr's Garage, and he had come to my rescue any number of times when I'd become so focused on a case that I'd run out of gas or locked my keys in my car. "There's some woman in the fun house who swears she just saw the ghost of Genie Martine in the mirror maze."

"Cool!" Scott bellowed. "Let's go see!"

He and Maggie zoomed off, leaving us in the dust—make that sawdust, which was strewn all over the ground. The scent reminded me of going to the circus as a little girl with my dad. The two older sisters rolled their eyes and George said, "Better that than the death coaster, I guess."

"Ooh, fun houses give me chills," Deirdre announced, swinging her Kewpie doll earrings at Ned and Charlie both.

I thought it was interesting that Deirdre was hanging out with us at all. We'd had a lot of years to establish that we didn't like each other much, and I wondered where her actual friends were. Now and then she'd resume her attempts to snag Ned, but I knew he was a one-girl-detective kind of guy.

He and I held hands as we maneuvered through the crowds, and then all six of us—Charlie included—came to a dead stop in front of the entrance to the fun house.

It was definitely chill-inducing—a large, black-and-green monster with red horns and glowing green eyes towered above the curved door, which was located where the monster's abdomen would be. Its wings extended on either side, spanning the length of the building. Terrible shrieks and eerie electronic music made the bones in my head vibrate. I wondered what my dad would think of it—it definitely wasn't the old-fashioned style of fun house he'd probably experienced when the first Cutter Brothers Funland occupied these grounds.

A Funland employee wearing a skeleton costume and a top hat unfastened the red velvet cord stretched across the entrance and ushered us in.

"No pushing, no shoving, and no going insane with fear," he said in a spooky voice.

"Maybe we should have stuck to the roller coaster," Bess whispered as we moved with about fifteen other people into the pitch-black interior.

There was an ear-piercing scream, followed by a flashing black light that revealed dozens of gargoyle faces leering down at us from the ceiling, bouncing up and down as if they were on bungee cords. Then air gusts blew up at us from the floor. Crazy laughter echoed all over the room and lights went out, throwing us into darkness. Next, strobe lights flickered, making our movements seem robotlike.

"This is so cool!" a voice shouted in my ear. It was Scott.

"Stay close," George warned him.

"Please. I'm not a baby," he shot back.

"Next stop, the mirror maze," Charlie said. "Haunted by the ghost of Genie Martine."

"If you stare into the mirror and say her name five times, she'll appear to you," Scott informed us.

"That's just an urban legend," George said. "Ghosts are not real."

"Bess believes in ghosts," Maggie announced. "She gets all scared during horror movies and then she can't sleep."

"Thank you for sharing," Bess said, laughing.

We exited the Gargoyle Room and walked past several panels of mirrors that distorted our images as colored lights flashed on and off: pencil-thin Ned-and-Nancy; stretched-out-in-the-middle George and Bess; teeny-weeny miniature Deirdre and Charlie; and way-bulgy-eyed Scott and Maggie.

Then we entered the mirror maze, a bewildering warren of mirrors and clear panels designed to completely confuse us. I saw Nick in front of me and walked toward him, only to collide with a thick glass barrier. We laughed and waved at each other, and both of us turned to the right. Six—or was it six hundred?—images of myself surrounded me, breaking apart like the shifting patterns of a kaleidoscope as I turned in a circle, hands outstretched. My hand brushed across mirrors and glass, and then nothing—aha, the next step forward!

Soon we were all literally bouncing off the walls and laughing—at least at first. I noticed that the lights were growing dimmer and the sound track featured a human heartbeat; we all began to concentrate a little harder on finding our way out, and I had the eeriest sense that I was being watched.

Well, of course you are, I told myself. There's probably an attendant monitoring the maze at all times. In fact, for all I knew, someone might be standing behind the mirrored wall directly in front of me. I stared at my own reflection, imagining someone else's eyes gazing back at me . . . Genie Martine's eyes, ghostly and white . . .

Stop it, I admonished myself.

"You okay?" Ned asked me, turning around in front of me and holding out his hand.

"Sure." I grinned at him. "Just working overtime to scare myself."

"Come *on*, you guys! We're the last ones in here!" Scott bellowed up ahead. I couldn't see him, but as I looked around, I realized he was right—I didn't see anyone else in the maze except for us.

"I want to get out of here," Deirdre whined. I glanced to my left as she seemed to appear out of thin air. "It's creeping me out."

I smacked my forehead. "I almost forgot! There's a trick to getting out of mazes. It's called the left-hand rule. Just put your hand on the surface to your left. If there's a space, keep following the barriers to the left. We'll eventually get out."

"That doesn't sound like it would work," Deirdre sniffed. "I'll do it my own way."

"Okay," I said, as Nick flashed me a quick little grin and placed his hand on the mirror to his left. We two began to move forward, always keeping contact with the left side. Within minutes, we stepped out of the maze to the sound of recorded applause and cheers.

The next thing we heard was an "Ooph!" followed by a thud. Ned and I traded looks and broke into a run, beneath black lights that made the white parts of our clothing glow a spectral purple.

We blasted past spooky figures from current monster movies toward an opened door surrounded by giggling bats. Just outside the exit, Scott sprawled on the ground, tangled up with an older man in a black pants and a red jacket with FUNLAND embroidered in yellow across the back. He was wearing mittens; a broom and a long-handled metal dustpan lay nearby. Maggie stood with her hands clasped in shock over her mouth.

"I'm sorry," Scott said, leaping to his feet. Maggie swooped down and grabbed the man's broom. "Are you okay?"

"Jackson's okay, him's okay," the man said as Ned darted forward and offered a hand. Getting up, he grabbed the dustpan and batted awkwardly at the broom. Through the mittens, I could see that his fingers were twisted and gnarled.

"Genie," he whispered, as he finally grabbed the broom.

Scott's eyes widened. "Have you seen her?"

The man—I assumed his name was Jackson—swallowed hard and nodded. "Her was crying," he replied. He shuffled away. "Sweep, sweep," he said.

"No way," Scott blurted. "Where?" He turned back around. "Did you hear that? He said he saw

Genie!" Scott was practically yelling. "Let's go back in!"

"No way," Maggie cut in, scowling as she put her arms around herself. "I'm not going back through that dumb maze again."

"You're scared!" Scott crowed. "Come *on*. This is our chance to see a real ghost!"

"He was just trying to freak you out," Maggie retorted.

"I'll go back through the maze with you," Ned told Scott, "if it's okay with your sister." He raised a brow at George.

"Please, I'm twelve," Scott grumbled, rolling his eyes.

"Yes, you may go," George replied pointedly. "If you promise not to run."

Ned and Scott walked back around to the front of the fun house and joined the line. Deirdre got a cell phone call and announced that her friends had arrived—implying, of course, that we were *not* her friends, but that was fine by me. Charlie hung out with us, then got a call to rescue a stranded motorist and left.

About half an hour later, Scott and Ned caught up with us at the dime-toss booth. People leaned over a barrier and threw coins onto cheap glass dishes, platters, and goblets. Superjock George had already scored a nice big stuffed purple unicorn and a frog that said "Ribbet!" when she squeezed his stomach.

"No ghost," Ned reported.

"Yes, ghost!" Scott insisted. "I saw her in one of the mirrors!"

"You did not," Maggie said. "You are so dramatic, Scott."

"*Me?*" he cried. "If anyone is a drama queen, it's you!"

As the two cousins started bickering, Ned smiled at me. "No ghost," he said quietly.

After that, we played a couple more booth games—Ned presented me with my own stuffed purple unicorn—and we rode a lot of rides, including the "death coaster," which was every bit as terrifying as it looked, and ate a lot of junk food.

"I have to get back to the *Bugle*," Ned told me. "I have some last-minute writing to do."

He gave me a quick kiss and loped off to the park exit. Next, we went to the pumpkin patch to choose good carving pumpkins for Halloween. The pumpkins were arranged in large groups on bales of hay and wooden carts. Scott picked one that looked as if it had deflated, and Maggie's was perfect and round. Eventually, we all headed for the Funland exit. There, we found Deirdre alone, looking very upset.

"Have you seen my earring?" she asked, pulling back her hair to reveal her bare left earlobe. She looked at Scott. "You went back through the maze, right? Did you see it?"

Scott shook his head, and Deirdre's shoulders slumped. "Those earring were one-of-a-kind," she said. "Irreplaceable."

"I can go back in and look for it," Scott volunteered.

Deirdre's eyes widened. "That'd be great," she said.

"Sorry," George interjected. "But these guys have to get home. They both have soccer in the morning." She made a face. "And it's my turn to drive them, so Maggie is staying at our house and Bess gets to sleep in."

Just then, a PA system came on.

"Hello, Funlanders! Funland will be closing in fifteen minutes! Fifteen minutes! Come back tomorrow and have some more fun!"

Deirdre frowned. I felt sorry for her; if I hadn't driven the group, I would have volunteered to help her look.

"Well, I'm going back," Deirdre said, taking off.

"Good luck," I replied, to her retreating back.

I dropped everyone off and went home. The delicious scent of freshly baked brownies would have normally tempted me to make a detour to the kitchen, but I was stuffed with nachos and popcorn. I quickly got ready for bed and dropped off to sleep.

The ring tone of my cell phone woke me up, and I hazily grabbed it out of my purse. The caller ID read SHANNON.

"Deirdre?" I asked, into the phone.

"No. This is her mother," Mrs. Shannon replied. "I was wondering if she was with you, Nancy. I called her earlier in the evening and she said she was with you at Funland."

I looked over at my alarm clock. It was after eleven. Funland had closed at ten.

"Well, actually, I left a while ago," I told her. "She was still there when we left. She was looking for her earring."

"Oh, that's just wonderful," Mrs. Shannon huffed angrily. "Those earrings were a special present from Belle Cutter, the new owner. My husband did all her legal work," she added self-importantly. "I told Deirdre they were too valuable to wear to an amusement park. Well, if you see her, please tell her to come home immediately."

"I will, Mrs. Shannon," I replied—to the dial tone. I decided to give her the benefit of the doubt—maybe she didn't realize how late it was, or that she had pretty much hung up on me.

I lay in bed for a few more minutes, wondering where Deirdre could be. It bothered me that I'd last seen her returning to the maze, and that she hadn't made it home. My detective's brain just couldn't let a loose end like that go.

I reached over to the drawer in my nightstand and pulled out my laptop. I instant-messaged both George and Bess to see if either of them was still up. Bess IM'ed back.

GLAMGRL: HI!
NDrew: OK 2 CALL U?

My phone rang.

"Hi," Bess said. "What's up?"

I quickly told her about Mrs. Shannon's call.

"Even though the Shannons have my cell phone number, I don't have Deirdre's," I said.

"Me neither, curse the luck," Bess retorted. "So you want to go back to Funland and see if she left, right? Because detectives just can't stand loose ends?" Without giving me time to answer, she went on. "And you want some company. And since I answered your IM, I volunteered myself."

I chuckled. "And you don't have soccer duty in the morning."

"And I'm the one who believes in ghosts, so of course I'm just the perfect one to drag back to a deserted amusement park in the middle of the night."

"You're right four times in a row," I replied cheerfully. "We'll look for her car in the lot. If we find it, we'll locate their security guard and ask for help," I promised.

"Why can't Mrs. Shannon look for her?" Bess grumbled. "Don't answer that. I know why. Because she's Mrs. Shannon."

"I'm pretty sure she thought we were still out somewhere. Probably because Deirdre still is."

"The things we do for people who aren't our friends," Bess grumbled.

I picked Bess up at her house. A late-night fog had rolled in, coating the familiar streets of our hometown with swirls of thick white mist. I turned on my low beams and moved slowly; luckily, there weren't many cars on the road. Everything looked different, covered with the heavy blankets of white.

We pulled into the parking lot and rolled

through the swirling mist searching for Deirdre's snazzy convertible. Eventually, we found it, looking conspicuous in the otherwise deserted lot.

"Maybe she's afraid to drive in this fog," I said.

We went over to the car and I knocked on the window. There was no response. I pulled my pencil flashlight from my purse and peered inside. As far I as could tell, the car was empty.

The sign over the entrance was turned off. After returning to my hybrid to get out a flashlight for Bess, I slung my purse over my shoulder and led the way to the closed ticket booth. Tall double metal gates stretched across the entrance, padlocked in place.

"Hello?" I called, passing my flashlights over the booths. No one answered. I whipped out my cell phone and called the phone number listed at the base of the signs posted on each booth. All I got was a recorded message giving me the hours of operation. There wasn't even a way to leave a message for them.

"Look," Bess said, moving past the ticket booth and playing her flashlight beam over a door beside one of the gates. It was ajar.

Before I could say anything, she went through it. I figured we'd find Deirdre and get her out of there, and no one would be the wiser regarding our trespassing on private property. I went in after Bess.

"Wow, this is really freaky," Bess said as we walked. Everything was very foggy and dark—much darker than I would have expected. Most businesses leave at least a few lights on at night for security reasons. The fog rolled on top of itself, then tumbled and spread out like breakers hitting a beach.

"The fun house is on the other side of the park," I said.

"Scott would love this," Bess sighed.

I'm a fairly levelheaded person, and I'm used to creeping around in the dark, but I had to admit that I wasn't loving being in Funland in the foggy darkness. As my flashlight played over smiling clown faces, the movements of the fog made them seem as if they were winking at us and moving their lips.

I got to thinking about Jackson, the man Scott and Maggie had knocked over. I wondered if he was out shambling in the dark. I couldn't believe he was any kind of threat—or rather, I didn't want to believe it. But at the moment, with the swirling shadows and our creepy surroundings, it was getting easier to believe that something bad had happened to Deirdre.

Soon we stood in front of the fun house, with its big, scary monster entrance looming above us. The rope across the front had been removed, and the door was hanging open. The fog swam in ahead of us.

"If we step inside, will we activate some kind of sensor?" Bess wondered anxiously.

I doubted we would get in trouble for looking for Deirdre—I had proof that I'd called Funland first, right on my cell phone. In fact, it might be a good thing if someone discovered us—they could help us look for her. And if it turned out that she was safe and sound, she probably wouldn't have to worry about repercussions, since her father had acted as the park's legal representative. Of course her parents might have a few choice words for her. . . .

"One way to find out," I said, and walked through the door into the pitch-black Gargoyle Room, playing my flashlight over the grotesque faces hanging from the ceiling and ringing the walls. Nothing happened, and I gestured over my shoulder for Bess to come on in.

"Deirdre?" I called.

"Shh!" Bess hissed. "Someone might hear you!"

"Yes, Deirdre might hear us," I said gently. "She may be hurt, Bess."

Bess grimaced. "I hope not."

"Me too."

We moved through the Gargoyle Room and entered the maze. Our flashlights bounced back at us. I aimed mine at a place in the floor just beyond the toes of my shoes so I could light my way without becoming blinded by the reflection of the beam. I extended my hand to the left, touching the nearest hard surface, and gestured for Bess to walk behind me and do the same.

"We'll get through the maze quickest by following the left-hand rule," I explained. I tried not to think about how that wouldn't solve our problem if Deirdre had wandered somewhere off in the maze, hit her head, and been knocked unconscious.

I took a breath to call out again.

Bess must have heard me; she put a hand on my shoulder and said, "Nancy, please don't. I'm really scared."

"Okay," I said. Then I moved forward, keeping my hand against the mirrored panel beside me. I walked forward; then my hand lost contact. I moved to the left, found the wall again, and made a sharp turn. Bess was right behind me. I kept going, shining the flashlight at my feet.

We twisted and turned, gliding steadily forward. I pulled out my cell phone to see how long we'd been inside the maze. Probably five minutes at most, but it seemed like a lot longer. Then we came upon a row of three mirrors.

"I recognize this part. This is the spot where Charlie said people have been seeing Genie Martine," Bess whispered. Her voice was tight and breathy.

Then I saw something that made my heart skip a beat: a tube of lip gloss lay on the floor, pushed up against the bottom of the barrier. I recognized it at once—it was Deirdre's expensive brand, lying in a field of broken glass. *Glass?* The hair on the back of my neck rose as I ran my flashlight beam across the floor, to discover that the lower section of mirror behind it was cracked and broken. Signs of a fall?

A struggle, more likely.

"Nancy?" Bess asked anxiously. "What's going on?"

I squatted down on my heels and reached in my purse for the pair of tweezers I always carry for collecting evidence. I also flicked open my cell phone. I had a direct line to the River Heights Police Department on speed dial, and I wouldn't hesitate to call them if I thought we were in danger. I bent forward to retrieve the lip gloss with my tweezers.

In the same instant, the panel behind me burst apart with a terrible crash, throwing me forward. I closed my hand around something sharp, dropping my chin to my chest as I yelled at Bess, "Glass! Look out!"

My flashlight and phone went flying as someone tackled me. Bess's answering shout was abruptly cut off. I struggled hard against my captor, my mind registering that what I was holding was a piece of glass.

I was about to shout to Bess when a hand covered my mouth and held me still.

"What did I tell you, huh?" a woman's harsh voice demanded in my ear. "I knew someone would come looking for that girl. "Now we have *three* girls."

Light mushroomed from behind me, reflecting in the panel in front of me. My captor was the ticket-booth lady with the long gray braids!

What is going on? I thought as she straightened, yanking me to my feet, still with her hand over my mouth.

I know self-defense, and I also had a weapon—a piece of glass—but I ticked my glance to see a very muscular guy around our age holding on to Bess. By his high cheekbones and thin lips, I judged him to be related to the woman—he might have been her son. I tried to signal Bess to fight, but her eyes were wide with panic, and she didn't even seem to see me. I made a plan B—I could get free and grab the phone, call the police . . .

Except that with the dim light surrounding me, I couldn't spot my cell phone. I glanced at Bess again, and this time she blinked at me. I blinked at her. She blinked back.

"What are we gonna do, Ma?" the guy asked, frowning. He looked almost as frightened as Bess.

The woman huffed. And then she blinked and leaned forward, craning her neck. She whooped and pointed at the floor.

"Beau, look!" she ordered him. "There's the earring!"

I followed where she was looking. About two feet to the left of Deirdre's lip gloss, her Kewpie-doll earring glittered among the pieces of glass.

"There it is," he said. He looked torn between holding on to Bess and picking up the earring. "Come with me," he said to Bess, walking her backward toward the broken panel. Their shoes crunched on the broken glass. I watched in the mirror as they went behind me and disappeared.

The woman must have sensed my tension; she frowned at my reflection and held her hand more tightly over my mouth.

"If you want to see your friend again, don't try anything," she snarled at me.

From behind us, the young man grumbled, "Hold still!"

About a minute later, he returned. Alone.

"I tied her up," he told the woman. Then he moved past us and fished Deirdre's earring out of the glass carefully. He either ignored the lip gloss or didn't see it as he held the little Kewpie doll like a tiny fish.

"That's it," the woman said eagerly. "Oh, glory be, at last!" She threw back her head. "Open it, Beau!"

As I watched, the young man—Beau—picked up Deirdre's valuable earring and cracked it in two. My captor watched him intently, gripping me painfully. Then Beau grunted and held up what looked to be a safe deposit key.

"That's it!" She laughed, sounding crazy. "Get some more rope and tie this one up too," she said. "Hurry. We have to get out of here."

That gave me hope that they would tie us

all up and then leave us in the maze. I made a fist, hiding the piece of glass while the woman turned me around and led me through the broken panel.

We were behind the mirror maze now, and the wall before me was nothing but a piece of plywood paneling. An electrician's lamp hung from the darkness above us, and in its bluish light, I saw Bess to my right. She was sitting on a metal folding chair, gagged with what appeared to be a dishtowel, and her hands tied in front of her.

Deirdre sat on an identical chair, gagged with a blue bandana, with her hands tied in front of her. Her eyes grew huge when she saw me, imploring me to help her. There was nothing I could do . . . at the moment, as Beau expertly bound my wrists. But I figured if I stayed calm and paid attention, I'd find an escape route for all three of us.

"Let's go," the woman said brusquely, as she leaned down and helped first Bess, and then Deirdre, to their feet. Deirdre whimpered.

They herded us single file past more paneling. I saw the angles of the maze and figured the reflective panels were actually one-way mirrors. If they'd been after Deirdre's earrings all along, they could have been watching for them ever since the park opened.

"I wish your granddad was here to see this," the woman said. "Justice at last."

I swallowed hard behind my gag, wondering what she meant.

Soon we were outside in the chill night air. The fog wrapped itself around us. I was in the lead, with Deirdre and Bess somewhere behind me. The white, full moon provided the only light as they led us outside the fun house; the fog obscured our vision more often than not. We walked past some bathrooms and the horseshoe-shaped food court where I had bought my nachos; the place had been locked up for the night. Bushes rustled as we passed.

"We have to get out of here. That guard will wake up soon," the woman muttered. "I should have put more of those tranquilizers in his coffee."

No security guard, I told myself. I hoped he would be all right.

A chain-link fence batted with a covering loomed in front of us. The woman fished in her jacket pocket and pulled out a ring of keys. A padlock dangled from a chain securing the door to the fence.

She glared at me.

"I have to let you go to unlock this," she said. "If you try to run, we'll take it out on your friends. Do you understand?"

I nodded, and stood unmoving as she jammed a key in the lock and opened it. She pushed the door open and motioned me through.

We stood in a field just outside the perimeter of Funland. Vines curled and I saw large round shapes lying among them. I smelled the earth and the scent of pumpkin, and I realized we were walking through a pumpkin patch—probably the same patch where Funland harvested their pumpkins to sell.

Across the patch, a black shadow rose like a crouching monster. The fog was too think for me to figure out what it was, but as we drew near, I realized it was a motor home. My stomach clenched but I stayed focused. I shivered in the cold as wind whistled around me. I might as well have been blindfolded; the fog was so intense.

We walked over vines and soggy earth. I heard a low wail—the wind, I told myself—but it sounded eerie and mournful.

"What is that?" Beau asked his mother.

"A dog," she snapped.

"Some people say they can hear Genie crying in the moonlight," Beau ventured.

"That's crazy talk."

The wailing continued. As the fog thinned slightly, I caught sight of Beau, looking around. His face was pale, and he looked like a ghost himself. He caught my eye and grimaced, almost as though he was making a little apology.

Maybe I can get him to help us, I thought. I turned my head, relieved to see Bess and Deirdre about five feet behind me, their eyes huge above their gags.

By then, we'd reached the motor home. There were two steps up to a door; the woman held on to my arm as she climbed them and opened the door, pulling me up beside her.

She led me into the dark interior.

"Sit down," she snapped, pulling on my hand and making me sit on what felt like a vinyl banquette with a table in front of me. My bound hands rested on my lap beneath the table.

"Hand up the other two," the woman said.

Deirdre sat next to me, followed by Bess. I saw their terrified expressions as Beau passed his flashlight beam across the three of us.

"No funny stuff," he ordered, looking almost as frightened as we were.

Beau and his mother walked off to my left. I followed them with my gaze, to see them flopping into the driver and passenger seats of the motor home. Oh, no, what if they drive off? I thought. Bess stared at me and Deirdre whimpered, and I could tell they were thinking the same thing.

"Let's go," Beau's mother said.

Deirdre whimpered again. I carefully opened my hand and started working the piece of glass toward my fingers. I knew I had to hurry before my hands went numb from the tightness of the rope. I nudged Deirdre just as the engine began to rumble and the headlights came on. I blinked at her. She hesitated, then blinked back. Good. She knew something was up.

"Turn off the headlights," the woman instructed Beau. "They won't help us in this fog and they'll just call attention to us."

The light around us dimmed. There was still a faint glow from the vehicle's instrument panel. I turned slightly to Deirdre and angled the piece of glass against her finger. She felt it and blinked at me, signaling that she understood. I pressed the shard against the rope around her wrists and began to saw. She blinked. Then she rocked her wrists quickly back and forth to help the sharp edge of the glass cut the fibers.

We make a good team, I thought, blinking in encouragement. Blinking back, she rocked faster.

"What are we going to do with them?" Beau asked his mother again.

"I don't know. It's your fault they're here," she shot back. "I *told* you to hurry up, but you had to go check on that security guard again."

"Ma, we put sleeping pills in his coffee. We could have hurt him."

She said nothing.

"We can let them go," he went on. "They don't know who we are."

Suddenly, the woman got out of her seat, picked up Beau's flashlight, and threaded her way back to us. I stopped sawing and sat facing straight ahead.

The angle at which she held the flashlight beneath her chin shot streams of light over her face, casting it in spooky hollows like someone telling a ghost story at a campfire. She held on to the table with her free hand and glared at the three of us.

"The way I see it, the minute you three tell anyone what you've seen so far, everyone will know who we are. No one ever listened to Daddy. So *I'm* going to make you girls listen to *me*."

"Ma," Beau called, his voice high and anxious, "is that really a good idea?"

"Daddy was innocent," she said fiercely. "He

only meant to scare Marty and Del Martine."

Martine? I thought, my sleuth brain taking notes. That was Genie's last name.

"Marty and Del Martine were brothers who worked for Cutter Brothers Funland the same time Daddy worked there. Daddy was in charge of the Spinner."

The Spinner? My stomach flipped. Genie Martine had died on the Spinner.

"The Martines were stealing money from the game booth they worked," she went on. "They would accept cash from players instead of tickets and keep it. They were robbing the Cutters blind."

"Ma, please," Beau said. "There's no need to tell them this stuff."

"Daddy found out," the woman continued. "He told them he wanted some of that money or he would report them to the Cutters. They said no. So Daddy threatened 'em a little, tried to scare 'em. Marty had that pretty daughter, Genie. Genie loved to ride the ride my dad ran for the Cutters—the Spinner. She rode it every day after school, two or three times."

Deirdre made a little sound behind her gag. The woman's gaze ticked toward her immediately.

"I know exactly what you're thinking," she

213

said. "You think my dad had something to do with her death. That he fixed it so the Spinner went out of control and killed her, because Marty and Del Martine refused to share."

It sounded logical to me. After all, she *had* died on the Spinner. . . .

"Well, it didn't happen that way!" She balled her fist and slammed it down on the table. All three of us jumped. "It was an accident. Genie was my friend. She was three months older than me, and we had the run of the park, two carnival kids. Do you actually think my daddy would do something like that to a friend of mine?"

I stared at her. Though her face was aged and lined, she was probably only eight or nine years older than my dad. Haggard and careworn, she was so fierce and angry that I wondered if she was entirely sane.

"Within days after she died, the Martines all left town. The Cutters said my father was to blame for Genie's death. They fired him and he got thrown in jail."

Her forehead wrinkled. "Lousy cheap lawyer. We didn't have money for a decent one. Eventually the case got thrown out but he was a ruined man by then. *My* life was ruined." She glared at us as if we had been the ones who had ruined it.

"Ma, please," Beau said again.

"I started looking for the Martines. I spent years looking for them. My whole life."

She smiled sourly. "Then I found Genie's dad in a rest home. Marty Martine was a wreck. He said he had been haunted his entire life. He said the ghost wouldn't leave him alone."

Deirdre whimpered again.

"He finally told me that right after Genie died, he and his brother Del decided that the money was cursed. They had been keeping the money in a safe deposit box in a bank. They hid the key in one of the prizes at their booth—a pair of Kewpie-doll earrings. Then they left town—and left the key behind too. I made Marty give me the address of the bank and the safe deposit box number. Then I started looking for those earrings. Never could find 'em."

And it was just Deirdre's luck to get that very pair of earrings as a gift, I thought.

"When Cutter Brothers reopened two months ago, I applied for a job. No one knew who I was, of course."

She smiled at me, looking a little crazy. My stomach did another flip and my hands began to shake so hard I was afraid I would drop the shard of glass.

"You can't deny that fate has had a hand in this whole thing," she said. "Beau and I deserve the money the Martines stole. And we're finally going to get it!"

"Ma, that's enough," Beau insisted. "The more you tell them, the more dangerous it is for us. Once we let them go, they'll tell the police everything."

The woman narrowed her eyes at us. She said in a very quiet voice, clearly not meant for her son to hear, "Then maybe we shouldn't let them go."

I felt a sharp thrill of fear. What was she saying?

She grinned again, then left us there and returned to her seat beside her son. I got back to work sawing Deirdre's rope. I heard a rhythmic back-and-forth sound farther down beneath the table, and I hoped it was Bess, working to free herself, too.

We rode along in silence for a long time as I worked like crazy. Deirdre kept blinking, and I'd blink back. Tears welled in her eyes and I gave my head a shake.

Don't lose hope, I tried to tell her. We're going to be okay.

"We should pull over," Beau told his mother. "It's too foggy to drive."

"No. We're going to Chicago *now*," she insisted. "As soon as that guard wakes up, and someone reports those missing girls, they'll start searching for them. We need to get to the bank as soon as it opens."

"Okay. But after we get the money, we'll let the girls go," he said.

His mom didn't answer.

I have no idea how long it took, but I finally did enough damage to Deirdre's rope that she could loosen it up and free her hands. She reached for her gag, but I shook my head to warn her to leave it. She worked on my rope, untying some knots and cutting through others. Finally, she got me free. My hands tingled painfully and I rubbed them to get the circulation back while Deirdre worked on Bess. She had managed to fray the rope a little, but she needed Deirdre's assistance to get all the way free.

By silent consent, we loosened our gags but kept them on for appearance's sake. My heart was hammering. I wasn't sure if Bess and Deirdre could see my gaze moving to the door's location and then back to us.

"Ma, I'm pulling over," Beau said. "It's just too foggy. What if we hit another car?"

"Oh, all right," his mother grumbled.

I took a huge chance and pulled down my gag. "Get up," I whispered urgently to the others. "As soon as he slows down, we're going to go out the door."

Deirdre reached behind her head and yanked down her gag. So did Bess.

The motor home shuddered as it rolled to a stop; we edged around the table and stumbled in the direction of the door. I found the knob and turned it, yanking the door open. I could only see fog as I jumped without making a sound!

Luckily, I landed in soft earth. Someone landed right next to me; there was a third thud, and I got to my feet and grunted, "Run!"

The fog washed over me and I crashed into dense foliage. Then the mists parted and thinned just enough for me to realize I had run into a row of cornstalks. We were in a cornfield! That was good; the tall rows of waving corn could provide us with lots of hiding places once Beau and his mother discovered that we had escaped.

"Come on!" I urged.

As we ran, the stalks rustled and cracked; the rounded furrows threw us off balance time and again. Deeper we went into the cornfield, and deeper still. For a few seconds, all I heard was the crash of my feet and my heavy panting. Corn tassels tickled my cheeks. My hands still hurt as blood pumped back into them. I wished I had my cell phone.

"Deirdre! Bess!" I whispered as loudly as I dared. "Do either one of you have your cell phone?"

"No! Nancy, Bess, where are you?" Deirdre half-shouted. "I can't see you!"

"They've escaped!" I heard the woman shout to the field. "You girls get back here now!"

Deirdre let out a little cry. Then the wind blew away layers of fog and I saw the stalks beside me shaking.

"Don't move," I told her, pushing my way through the row. I came out the other side in front of her. Bess crashed through the next row over, and we were reunited.

I turned around and gazed back in the direction of the motor home. The fog had thinned again, and I saw the woman with her flashlight, scanning the rows of corn. Any second, she would see us. What would she do then? Would Beau come after us?

"*There* you are!" she shrieked.

I braced myself . . . and then she ran off in the exact opposite direction, away to our left.

I couldn't believe our luck. I waited to see if

Beau followed after her, but he didn't appear. I figured he was still in the motor home. Then I remembered the old dirt bike strapped to the rear of the vehicle. We could double back, grab it, and one of us could go for help. . . .

"Maybe they'll just drive on to Chicago," Deirdre said hopefully, "and forget about us. If we're stranded out here . . ."

"Ma, come on, let's go!" Beau bellowed from the motor home.

"Not without them," she insisted. "Not if I have to look for them all night!"

"Does that answer your question?" Bess asked Deirdre, who grimaced.

"*There* you are!" If anything, her voice was farther away.

"She's following something, but it's not us," I said. "Maybe it's a raccoon or something."

"I highly doubt she could mistake *me* for a raccoon," Deirdre huffed.

"In the dark, she could," I said. "There's a dirt bike tied to the back of the motor home. If we can get to it, one of us can ride for help."

"Okay, Nancy," Bess said.

"No way. That's crazy," Deirdre argued.

I didn't say anything. I knew my plan was risky, and it was still possible that our kidnappers might eventually give up and drive away. Their plan had certainly spun out of control. Maybe Beau would be able to talk his mother into abandoning their scheme. That seemed like wishful thinking, though. From what I could tell, her bitterness and hard life had driven her a little crazy.

"Come back here!" the woman yelled, from even further away. And I had a thought . . . it was almost as if whatever she was chasing was luring her away from the motor home, deeper into the cornfield. As if it were trying to help us . . .

Now who's thinking like a crazy person? I chided myself.

The moon moved across the sky, occasionally hidden by clouds, as we crept up on the rear of the vehicle. A couple of times Deirdre announced that she was *not* budging one more inch closer, but as Bess and I left her behind, she scrabbled along to catch back up with us.

As I hid behind stalks of corn, I studied the dirt bike. As far as I could tell, it had been secured to the wheel only by bungee cords—easy to whip off. Bess joined me.

"I can probably hotwire that," Bess said. She's a wiz at anything mechanical—a real Ms. Fix-It.

"Ma, where are you?" Beau called. "Come on, let's just go!"

I closed my eyes and willed him to leave the vehicle in search of his mother. We could jump in, lock all the doors, and surely find a cell phone somewhere to call 911.

But as far as I could tell, he was still in the motor home—dangerously close to us. I crept from the safety of the cornfield to the berm where the dirt met the blacktop road. Bess tip-toed up next, and then, finally, a very reluctant Deirdre. We made short work of dislodging the dirt bike and setting it down.

"How are all three of us going to ride this?" Deirdre asked. It was a good question.

Bess said, "Nancy, you take it and ride for help."

"*What?*" Deirdre whispered. "And leave us here?"

"We can't all three ride it," Bess said. "If she goes for help, we have a chance."

"No," Deirdre protested. "That woman will go berserk when she finds out Nancy's gone."

"Beau, come out here and help me! They're over here!" the woman shouted from somewhere in the cornfield. The cornstalks were waving and dipping as she crashed around, but they were so tall I couldn't see her.

222

I glanced over as Beau came around the front of the motor home and peered out at the cornfield. Then he started to jog along the side of the vehicle—toward the rear . . . and *us*!

"Uh-oh," I whispered. "Bess, can you get it going?"

"I'll try." Bess crouched on one knee—just as Beau appeared behind her.

Deirdre sucked in her breath. Bess straightened. I looked at him. He looked at me.

"Please, let us go," I pleaded. "You know this isn't right."

His forehead furrowed with pain. "We've lived on the road all my life," he said. "If we can get that money . . ."

"Beau!" the woman called. "I've found the one with the auburn hair! Come *on*!"

"What is she talking about?" Deirdre demanded. "Nancy's right here!"

Beau looked confused too.

"Your mom is under a lot of stress," I said gently. "You know this isn't going to work out the way she wants it to." I gestured to Deirdre. "*Her* mother asked me to check on her. That's why we were at Funland after it closed. People are probably already looking for us."

Beau grimaced. "I'm sorry about all this."

"My mom called *you*?" Deirdre asked, sounding surprised.

"Beau! She's getting away!"

A row of cornstalks closer to us rustled and dipped. Beau groaned. Then he nodded. "Okay," he said. "Here." He fished in his pocket and pulled out the keys. He handed them to me. "The starter's tricky."

"Thanks," I said, swallowing hard. I'd never driven a motor home before.

I jogged around the driver side of the motor home, Bess and Deirdre close behind. As I opened the door, I heard the motor bike whirr to life. I jerked and looked questioningly at Bess.

"He must have the key," she said. "I didn't start it."

As we barreled into the motor home, the motorbike engine whined as if the bike were moving away from us.

"Maybe he's going for help too," Deirdre suggested. She was peering through the window beside the door.

"Make sure that's locked," Bess yelled as she plopped into the passenger seat. "Nancy, go!"

I jammed the key into the ignition. The engine turned over.

"Yes!" I bellowed. I floored it. "Look for a

phone, Bess. Hey, Deirdre, do you see a phone?"
I called.

"No." She walked up between the seats as I carefully hung a U—maybe not the safest maneuver, but I wanted to get back to River Heights in the worst way.

"No," Deirdre said again. Her voice was low and frightened. "I don't see a phone, and I don't believe I saw what I just saw, either."

"What?" Bess asked.

Deirdre licked her lips. "It's so strange, but Beau and his mom are chasing the motorbike."

I laughed. "That must be a sight, seeing them run after a riderless bike!"

"The pedal must have jammed down somehow," Bess theorized. "Maybe Beau did it to distract his mother so we could get away."

"It's not riderless," Deirdre said.

I took my eyes off the foggy, deserted road for an instant and looked at Deirdre in the rearview mirror. Her eyes were enormous and her face was chalk white.

"What do you mean?" I asked her.

"There's someone on it." Deirdre's voice shook.

"I don't get it," Bess said. "Who?"

Deirdre gazed at me. "You, Nancy. You're on it."

225

★★★★

We didn't talk much as I drove the motor home along the dark, foggy road. Deirdre was too shaken; Bess and I really didn't know what to make of what she'd said. I figured the fog had clouded her vision; most likely, Beau had been riding the bike toward his mom after all. Moonlight bleached colors; no one would have been able to make out my trademark auburn hair.

We couldn't find a phone anywhere, but while she was looking for it, Bess found Deirdre's earring, the key, *and* a slip of paper. It said, "Chicago First Mercantile Bank." There was an address, and a number. We figured that for the safe deposit box.

"Which way?" I asked, as we reached a fork in the road. Since we hadn't been able to see where the motor home was traveling, I didn't know how to get back to town. "If we see a light anywhere, even a car, we need to stop and ask for help."

"You got it," Deirdre said.

Then there was a pressure on my right wrist. I turned to Bess and asked, "Are you telling me to go right?"

Bess cocked her head. She wasn't touching me. But something was.

I swallowed hard.

Then there was pressure on my *left* wrist. Up ahead, there was an intersection.

"Am I supposed to go left?" I said aloud.

"Nancy, I don't know," Bess said apologetically. "I don't know the way back."

I licked my lips. "I'm not asking you, Bess," I said. "You guys, there's something in here with us."

"Like *what*?" Deirdre asked shrilly.

"I don't know, but it wants to help us get home," I answered.

Outside there was a sign that read CUTTER BROTHERS FUNLAND. An arrow pointed to the left.

I turned left, and saw the black shadow of the Ferris wheel rising into the sky. We started cheering.

And just then, three River Heights PD cars raced toward us with red-and-blue lights flashing in the murky mist. I flashed the brights and honked the horn, pulling over to the side as the police cars swarmed in tight formation.

I threw open the driver's door and poked out my head.

"It's Nancy!" I shouted. "Nancy Drew! We're safe!"

Chief McGinnis leaped out of the closest squad

car as officers surrounded the motor home. "Are the Dillards with you?"

Dillard, I thought. Beau Dillard.

"We left them in a cornfield," I said. "I'll show you."

"It's over, it's over, it's over!" Deirdre cried, reaching around my seat and hugging me. Hugging *me*.

"Okay, that's almost scarier than riding with a ghost," Bess whispered, as we got out of the vehicle. She gazed at me. "Is that what you meant?"

"I think so," I told her.

We stared at each other.

"It was smart of you to write down the license plate of the motor home on the fun house mirror," Chief McGinnis said.

"What?" I asked. I looked at Bess and Deirdre. They shrugged and looked back at me.

Chief McGinnis said he didn't need me to accompany him to the cornfield. I described the route I had driven in the motor home and he and all but one of his officers roared away. That Officer—Officer Rees—drove me to my hybrid, then followed me home.

Deirdre's folks were overjoyed to see her, and Mrs. Shannon assured me I would not be sued even though I had put Deirdre "in harm's way."

I called my dad, and he insisted he would be home on the next flight out. He arrived in the morning and he hugged me so tightly I couldn't catch my breath.

And I hugged him even tighter.

Then, a few hours later, Chief McGinnis gave me a call. He told me that the Dillards were in custody. Beau's mom, Thelma, had pled guilty to a long list of charges. I explained how Beau had helped us, and that I would be happy to testify to that in court.

I had already told Chief McGinnis about the earring, the key, and the slip of paper, which he retrieved.

"A judge approved the opening of the safe deposit box at the Chicago Mercantile Bank," he informed me. "You're not going to guess what was in it, Nancy."

"A lot of money," I informed him, sure of the answer.

"Nope. No money. A confession."

"What?" I gazed from the phone to my dad, who was listening on our extension.

"Yes," Chief McGinnis replied. "What Thelma Dillard told you is true . . . as far as it went. The Martines were stealing money from Funland, and

Sam Dillard—Thelma's father—tried to black-mail them for part of their ill-gotten gains." He paused.

"I'm with you so far," I assured him.

"Well, it seems that Genie Martine's Uncle Del is the one who jimmied the Spinner. He figured when the Spinner broke, Sam Dillard would be blamed, getting their potential blackmailer fired and providing a distraction while the Martines left town."

"Whoa," I blurted. "So Thelma was right. Her dad was innocent."

"Yes. The Spinner went completely out of control—it was a much worse accident than Del had tried to engineer. Genie died. And Del Martine never told a soul that he was responsible. He snuck to the bank and took all the money out of the safe deposit box. He left it on the steps of a church, and replaced it with the confession."

"But why hide the key?"

"Marty was the one who hid it in the earring. He didn't know that Del had already gotten rid of the 'cursed' money. And Del wasn't talking."

I gaped at my father, who sighed and shook his head. "The desperate act of a desperate man."

"Del and Marty Martine are gone, but Sam Dillard's still alive," Chief McGinnis said. "I've already got a call in to the nursing home where he lives. I'm going to tell him his name has been cleared. Belle Cutter's going to visit him. And she'd love to talk to you."

Later that afternoon, George, Bess, Deirdre, my dad, and I went to Funland to see Belle Cutter. The park wasn't yet open for the day, and walking through the grounds gave me an eerie sensation all over again.

The petite, pixie-faced owner of Funland recognized Deirdre, of course, but the rest of us were new to her.

"Tell me again what happened," she urged us.

"I still don't know how my earring went missing," Deirdre said. "It was like someone just lifted it off my ear inside the maze! And then those terrible people tied me up. And then Bess and Nancy came . . ."

"Looking for you, yes," Belle said.

"Then, in the cornfield, Thelma kept following someone, but it wasn't us. She said it was Nancy, but Nancy was with us. And then . . ."

Deirdre took a deep breath. "Then I saw someone riding the motorbike to distract the Dillards, and I thought it was Nancy. But there was no one else around for miles . . ."

We all looked quietly at each other. "I think it's very strange that the exact pair of earrings containing the key to that safe deposit box survived being in storage for forty years," Belle said slowly, cocking her head. "It's almost as if someone wanted them to be found."

"And someone wanted to keep us safe in the cornfield," Bess added.

And someone helped me find my way back to Funland, I thought.

"I need to show you something else," Belle said. "I think Chief McGinnis mentioned to you that the license plate of the Dillards' motor home was written on a mirror in the maze."

"Yes, I'd like to see that," I said.

We left Belle's office. We walked slowly past the exit to the fun house, and I saw Jackson, sweeping away, his gnarled hands wrapped around his broom. He smiled when he saw me and gestured for us to come inside with him.

"C'mere, c'mere," he said. "Come and see."

He turned and led the way back through the exit, into the maze. He knew the way by heart, and led us to the broken panel, where Thelma and Beau had attacked us. On an unbroken mirror beside it, the license plate of the motor home had been written in Deirdre's expensive lip gloss.

And beneath it, the words THANK YOU were written in the same handwriting.

"That 'thank you' wasn't there before," Belle mused.

"And look at this!" Deirdre dropped to a crouch and pointed.

Her lip gloss was on the floor, and beside it . . . another pair of Kewpie-doll earrings, worn with age, but still intact.

"I seen Genie," Jackson said, pointing at the THANK YOU. "Her was smiling."

THE END

CAROLYN KEENE

NANCY DREW

GIRL DETECTIVE™

Think Nancy's done solving crimes? Think again!

Now, Nancy's got a brand-new look—and triple the mystery on her hands! Collect all of the books in the new Nancy Drew: Girl Detective Perfect Mystery Trilogy:

  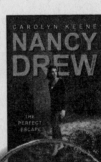

Pageant Perfect Crime 1-4169-5528-3
Perfect Cover 1-4169-5530-5

Coming Soon
The Perfect Escape 1-4169-5531-3